Desire by Design

Paula Altenburg

Also by Paula Altenburg

THE DEMON'S DAUGHTER

This book is a work of fiction. Names, characters, places, and incidents are the product of the author's imagination or are used fictitiously. Any resemblance to actual events, locales, or persons, living or dead, is coincidental.

Copyright © 2013 by Paula Altenburg. All rights reserved, including the right to reproduce, distribute, or transmit in any form or by any means. For information regarding subsidiary rights, please contact the Publisher.

Entangled Publishing, LLC
2614 South Timberline Road
Suite 109
Fort Collins, CO 80525
Visit our website at www.entangledpublishing.com.

Bliss is an imprint of Entangled Publishing, LLC. For more information on our titles, visit www.entangledpublishing.com.

Edited by Danielle Poiesz
Cover design by Jessica Cantor

Ebook ISBN   978-1-62266-100-8
Print ISBN   978-1-49376-236-1

Manufactured in the United States of America

First Edition May 2013

The author acknowledges the copyrighted or trademarked status and trademark owners of the following wordmarks mentioned in this work of fiction: Blackberry, Demerol, Disney World, Google, *GQ*, Gyprock, Jockey, Lycra, NASA, Peter Pan, Port-a-Potty, Prince Charming, Royal Canadian Mounted Police, Starbucks,

Superwoman, Superman, Tinker Bell, Victoria's Secret.

For Adeena

Chapter One

Evangeline Doucette tipped back in her office chair, closed her eyes, and plotted the mayor's assassination.

While she'd never actually act on it—she felt certain—plotting it was her personal form of therapy. Mayor Bob Anderson was one of the few people she'd ever worked with who completely ignored the fact that once a bid for the work was accepted and the contract signed, there was a budget that needed to be followed. It was a little frightening to think of him running a city, although it certainly explained a few things to Eve. Did City Council even know how many changes to the new City Hall design he'd already authorized?

As a project manager for Sullivan Construction, the company that won the tender for the new building, it was her job to keep the stakeholders informed of any risks and budget concerns. She'd tried, but it didn't help that her boss, Connor Sullivan, was good friends with the mayor—he didn't seem to want to listen to her concerns, either.

"It will all work out, Eve," Connor had said when she'd brought it up at their last meeting.

But *it will all work out* wasn't a good risk-management strategy, and Eve had a lot riding on this upcoming project.

She was one of the few project managers in the region who was also a qualified draftsman, and since the City Hall project was a design/build contract, Connor had placed her in charge of the design. In fact, she'd even drawn up the preliminary blueprints they'd sent in with the response to the tender.

The same ones the mayor kept changing.

A shrill wolf-whistle from outside jarred her concentration and brought her back to Sullivan Construction's current project, a new federal government office tower. Eve's eyes popped open, and her chair's front legs thudded to the floor. Leaning over, she peered beneath mini-blinds that were keeping the hot afternoon sun from beating into the stuffy, portable trailer that served as the on-site headquarters.

A few of the crew had gathered around a low stone wall overlooking the quiet Halifax side street. An attractive young woman in a short Lycra skirt and skin-tight halter-top was scurrying down the opposite sidewalk from the construction site, pretending to ignore her appreciative audience.

Eve muttered under her breath. Leaping from her chair, she yanked open the trailer door, stepped out into bright afternoon sunshine, and marched toward her crew.

"Hey," she called to the gathered men.

The young woman on the street was forgotten as they turned, en masse, and Eve had to work hard not to smile at the sea of repentant expressions before her. She'd seen those same looks before, yet it never made a bit of difference.

She folded her arms across her chest and tried to add a few extra inches to her overall height—which would still leave her by far the shortest person in the group. They might not mean any harm, but they had no idea how it felt to be a woman on the receiving end of their enthusiastic attention. This had to stop.

"Guys, I'm tired of fielding complaints because you harass

every woman who goes by," she said. "What if that were your wife or daughter? How would you like it then? Would you find it as amusing if I whistled at all the men who went by on the street? Or at *you*?"

As luck would have it, Eve spied a good-looking and attractive example approaching. There was a chin-up, eyes-forward purposefulness to him that spoke of someone comfortable with his own masculinity. He had the whole tall, dark, and handsome thing working for him in a way that caught her eye and made her look twice. While she couldn't see the finer details from this distance, he had short black hair, cropped close on the sides with a bit of curl to it on top, and an angular, even-featured face that no doubt photographed well.

Definitely worth that second glance. He didn't look like the type who'd need to whistle at a woman to get her attention. Not in that expensive, probably Italian, suit. No, more likely he'd have most women wanting to whistle at him.

Well, why not?

She elbowed her way through the crew, pushed up her checked-flannel shirtsleeves, and leaned over the short stone barrier.

"Hey, baby!" She punctuated her words with a wolf-whistle of her own that would have made her brothers proud. "Bring some of that over here!" She didn't bother taking note of the stranger's reaction but whirled back to face the speechless crew so she could finish her lecture. "It doesn't sound very attractive coming from me, does it?"

The burly foreman shrugged his hairy shoulders and gave her a gap-toothed grin. "Actually, it's kind of a turn-on."

She might have known she was wasting her time trying to prove a point to this group.

"Jeez, Eve," one of the carpenters complained. "First you paint mustaches on all the girls in the Port-a-Potty calendar, then you mark which ones have implants. Now, you won't let us admire what's right under our noses?" He cast a wistful look down the street, but the girl in the halter-top had disappeared around a corner. "And I'm pretty sure those weren't implants, either."

True, Eve had defaced their calendar. But only because they hadn't noticed that there was a woman working on-site who had to use that Port-a-Potty, too. To them, she was just a really short, skinny guy.

Without implants.

She dropped her hands to her hips and offered a compromise. "Tell you what... If you guys stop with the whistling, I'll quit drawing on the calendar."

Having established a mutually satisfying agreement, Eve hiked back to the trailer, repositioned herself in her chair, and propped her size-five, steel-toed work boots on the battered desktop. She twirled a studded earring in a nervous habit she couldn't seem to break. She had more important things to worry about than men being boys on a job site. She had to submit an update on the status of this nearly completed federal project, which was why she was on a construction site today and not in her office at Sullivan Construction.

She also had to straighten out the mess Halifax's megalomaniac mayor was making of the upcoming City Hall project. *Just another day in the life*, she thought. She'd had high hopes that her role as designer on the City Hall building would lead to more complex projects when it was finished. She already ran a nice little side business designing and renovating upscale private homes. At twenty-nine years of age—and as a woman in a male-dominated industry—those were no small achievements.

But Bob Anderson didn't seem to agree and was driving her nuts with his input. Worse, he kept volunteering her for pro bono charity projects around the city as if she were his personal construction assistant and she had nothing better to do with her spare time. At the moment, he had her working on renovations for an Internet café for teens. How could she say no to helping out with a youth program?

Killing Bob might be her only means of escape.

She sighed and turned her attention back to her computer screen, the work crew and the handsome guy in the Italian suit already forgotten.

...

Matt Brison had been around enough construction sites throughout his career that not much about them surprised him anymore, but having one of the workers whistle at him was a definite first.

At least she was cute. He wondered if that was the "annoying as hell" project manager he'd been hearing so much about from his uncle. If so, she had quite the rapport with the crew...and would be an interesting nut to crack.

His steps slowed as he neared the wall separating the construction site from the rest of the world, and he forgot all about being whistled at as he took in the project. He scanned the new four-story, ironstone structure with an architect's eye. It was staid, refined, and predictable, and without a doubt, suited its genteel, Georgian surroundings. Oak trees lined the neighborhood streets, filtering sunlight and shading sidewalks. Enormous lilac bushes sprawled against rolling green lawns, and the tangy scent of fresh-cut grass lingered on the thick, humid air.

Matt rubbed his forehead with the back of his hand. While he admired the historic feel of Halifax, his international reputation was based on modern, innovative design. Honesty compelled him to admit that his work wasn't suitable for this small, East Coast seaport. He wished with all his might that he'd been able to say no when asked to design its new City Hall, but his uncle never asked Matt for favors, so the project must be important to him.

"We want to bring Halifax into the twenty-first century," he had said when he'd asked Matt to fly down from Toronto and meet with the construction company that had been given the contract. "We want the world to know we're moving forward into the future. And you're just the man to prove it. I wouldn't trust it to anyone else."

The sentiment was perhaps admirable—and flattery was always nice—but Matt wasn't sure the future was where Halifax, Nova Scotia wanted to be. Anything he designed was going to stick out like a sore thumb in a city that dated back to the 1700s, and whose tourism industry relied heavily on promoting its Historic Properties district. He had visions of the Nova Scotia Association of Architects picketing the project.

Matt headed for the small office trailer near the entrance to the construction site, where all visitors were required to check in. He knocked on the door, then pushed it open when a woman called out, "Come in."

It took his eyes a second to adjust to the dingy, ill-lit interior. At first glance, there didn't even seem to be anyone inside. A drafting table stood in one corner, with a battered desk and laptop in another. There was a slight movement in the shadows, and he bent over to peer beneath the desk, where he was treated to the sight of a well-rounded, and very feminine, denim-clad posterior. Matt recognized the shirttail covering it.

He contemplated his opening line. *Hey baby, I brought it—where would you like me to put it?*

"Hello," he said, opting for a more professional greeting.

The sound of something connecting with the underside of solid wood made him wince. Her head popped up on the other side of the desk, and velvety brown eyes widened in recognition as they met his. A slim hand rubbed the back of a mass of coppery, auburn hair tied in a long, thick braid. Stray wisps clung to her cheeks. With her other hand, she held up a tiny object.

"Sorry. I dropped the back of my earring," she said.

Her soft voice made the nape of his neck tingle. Matt had to work hard not to smile. This wasn't at all the type of woman who'd need to whistle at strange men to get their attention. He watched in growing fascination as she slipped her earring back in place, then extended a hand to him. She had a firm, no-nonsense grip—he liked that in a woman.

"Well, this is awkward." Her cheeks flushed a pretty pink. "Eve Doucette, project manager."

"Matt Brison. Bob Anderson told me I might find you here."

Dismay crossed her face, and he wondered if she recognized his name. If so, she didn't seem like a big fan of his work.

"Sorry for that little incident outside," she said. "I was trying to prove a point to the men and made an error in judgment."

He felt a flicker of sympathy. Being a woman giving orders to a bunch of men on a construction site couldn't be easy. He didn't blame her for wanting to fit in with the guys.

Besides, she really was cute.

He pasted on his best smile and let a little interest slip into his eyes. "No need for apologies. I was flattered by the attention."

Her expression cooled, wariness creeping like a shadow over her face. It seemed she wasn't into flirtation. Duly noted. He wondered if that was because she was married. He checked. No ring.

Then, he examined her more closely.

She wasn't very tall. Matt estimated she stood about as high as his shoulder, but then again, he was a big man. Her skin was olive-hued and looked as if it might tan easily. She was thin—too thin, really—and her wide, long-lashed eyes had dark smudges under them, an indication she probably worked too hard. That wasn't unusual in an industry that often demanded twenty-three of the twenty-four hours available each day. Based on her job, she had to be in her mid-to-late twenties, but if he had to guess at her age on appearance alone, he'd swear she was too young to drink.

All things considered, she was attractive—in a wholesome, girl-next-door kind of way. Sexy, if one was attracted to the type.

He definitely could be. Lately, though, he'd taken to assessing the women he met for more than their sexual potential. That was still important, of course. At thirty-five, he wasn't dead. But he was starting to think about his future and where he saw himself by the time he was forty—and who he'd be sharing his success with. His ideal woman would be more comfortable in an evening gown than a hard hat—although that might be classed more as a job requirement than a priority since Matt entertained clients a lot. And she'd have to make a great mother because he wanted lots of kids. Being an only child had sucked.

And while Eve Doucette was cute—he was a sucker for big brown eyes, too—she didn't seem the right type. Besides, they had to work together. Then there were his uncle's warnings: *"Watch out for her, Mattie. She's all about the work, plain and simple. There's no reasoning with her once she gets an idea in her head. It's her way or the highway."*

He looked over at her. Okay, she was sending off huge I'm-unavailable-so-don't-waste-your-time vibes. That answered that. Matt might as well get right down to business.

"I wanted to touch base with you before I start on the new design for City Hall," he said. "Since we'll be working closely together, I thought we should meet. I'm the architect," he added, since she wasn't acting like she knew who he was.

Which knocked his ego down to size. He'd won major international awards and owned one of the most successful architectural firms in Canada. He couldn't recall the last time his name wasn't recognized by someone who worked in the industry.

"I know who you are," she said. "But I'm afraid I don't understand why you're here." She indicated a gray steel, tubular chair across from her desk, and he took a seat. She then skewered him with a steady, penetrating gaze that brought to mind his third-grade teacher, the one who'd caught him sticking a wad of chewed gum in Missy Parsons' gym sneaker. "I thought the draftsman who did the preliminaries would be doing the final design."

"City Council decided they want to hire a professional. Besides," he said with a shrug, "the final blueprints would need to be stamped by a licensed architect anyway."

Eve's pretty brow furrowed in a way that didn't bode well. Matt made a mental note to thank his uncle for giving him the job of messenger, since it was apparent no one at Sullivan Construction had spoken to her about him yet. He hated being the bearer of bad news, and he was fairly confident that Eve would consider this very bad news, indeed. Even though he was doing it as a favor to his uncle, he couldn't work for free, and his price tag was going to be a lot higher than some local draftsman's. That meant she was going to have to redo much of the cost analyses and budget. And the look on her face already indicated her feelings on the matter.

This truly was third grade all over again—except the wad of gum was a set of blueprints, Missy Parsons was an angry project manager, and somehow, Matt doubted that offering to share his granola bar at recess would make an adequate peace offering.

Uncle Bob might want to launch the city into the twenty-first century, but right now Eve Doucette looked ready to launch Matt a little farther.

His words might have been delivered in a foreign language for all the good they did Eve.

She'd spent weeks working on a budget for Sullivan Construction's proposal, and her plan didn't allow for hiring someone like Matt Brison. She'd wanted so much to do the design herself. It had been offered to her, even if unofficially. While she understood that preliminary designs were only meant to provide cost estimates on a design/build project, and that the final design often ended up being much different from what was submitted, the one she'd drawn up had been well received. So what on earth was Connor Sullivan thinking, agreeing to this?

It was like hiring Van Gogh to paint a garage, Henry Ford to design a go-cart, or Veronica Tennant to choreograph an elementary school dance recital.

"But I thought…" She tried not to sound hostile. "There must be some mistake. Surely you can see you're all wrong for this project."

"Oh?" He edged forward in his chair, suddenly intent, and the tiny trailer got even smaller. "Why do you say that?"

He had very blue eyes that never wavered from hers, as if

he were reading her thoughts, which was distracting.

Because her thoughts veered off in an unsettling direction she hadn't expected...and didn't want him to know.

That, coupled with deep disappointment, made her speak with even less tact than usual. "Your work is very modern. Abstract, in fact. You use a lot of glass and round edges. While your designs may have their place, I don't think the downtown district of Halifax is quite ready for them."

Let him chew on that. Eve hated most of his work, although she acknowledged it wasn't without merit. The modernist project he'd designed in Brussels had been an excellent example of practicality. She could appreciate practical.

She just didn't like modernist.

"And what do you think might be the appropriate style for this particular project?" he asked.

The neutrality of his tone, combined with his unwavering attention, set off an alarm in the back of her head. She wasn't sure if he was genuinely interested in her opinion or giving her just enough leeway to showcase her ignorance. Did he assume she didn't know what she was talking about simply because she didn't have a few extra letters after her name?

She counted to ten. More than once she'd been accused of being overly sensitive about her lack of a degree. She had an ex-husband with a PhD in Biology who used to make fun of her lower level of education to thank for that particular insecurity. It was one of the reasons he was now an ex. But this was not the time for her to get defensive or back down. She had done the research and was comfortable with her facts. Plus, there was nothing wrong with her design for the new City Hall. Her hackles started to rise, though she tried to tamp them down.

They want to hire a professional, indeed. Arrogant ass. She *was* a professional. And a darn good one.

She caught his eye and held his gaze, which turned out to be a mistake. He had a thick fringe of black lashes around those amazing blue eyes.

He was waiting for her to say something. She searched for her tongue.

"Second Empire," she stated. "Monumental, but not too flashy. Maybe with Georgian columns and simple arches, similar to what we've used on this site." She gestured toward the door and the building under construction outside. Then she shifted in her chair and tapped her fingertips on its wooden armrest. "That's what I did on the preliminaries, and it was exactly what the city wanted." She paused a minute to let it sink in, but his expression didn't shift. "Mr. Brison, did you even look at the preliminary plans? Have you even bothered to visit the city's Historic Properties district?"

"Yes to both. And please, call me Matt."

That good-natured, *GQ* smile of his made it harder for her to pull two thoughts together. He was smooth, she'd give him that, but some lessons were learned the hard way, and she knew better than to trust any man at the top of his field. Especially one who was being so nice. *Fool me once, shame on you. Fool me twice....*

She cleared her throat. "Well, Matt. Do you agree with me or not? Do you really think your work will suit the style of the district?"

A fleeting expression she couldn't identify crossed his face and was gone, and the easy smile was back in place fast. He would make a good poker player.

"I think my work will make a statement."

Eve couldn't resist. "It'll say, 'Help. I don't belong here. Find me a Starbucks.'"

A dark eyebrow went up. "Or it might say, 'Look at me. I'm a trendsetter, and in a class all my own.'"

"The poor thing will be lonely. We wouldn't want that." She took a deep breath and reminded herself that this was hardly his fault. He'd been asked to come here. She doubted very much that he'd begged for the opportunity. "I can straighten this out with a few phone calls. That way we won't be wasting any more of our time." She reached for the telephone. "Who hired you?"

"Bob Anderson approached me."

Of course. The mayor. Eve's assassination plot was looking more and more attractive by the second.

"That would explain it," she said. "The mayor is a moron."

Matt's easy expression never changed. "Maybe so. But that moron is my uncle."

Heat scorched her cheeks. She needed to learn to think first before she flipped the operating switch on her mouth.

"Perhaps 'moron' is too strong a word," she amended, nearly choking on the retraction.

A flash of humor curled the corners of his firm, full mouth. "He speaks highly of you, too."

Eve could well imagine. She recalled her last two conversations with the mayor without fondness. Bob considered himself a visionary. Eve thought his opinion of himself was overrated, unless by *visionary*, he meant *delusional*. He wanted City Hall to look like a giant sail. She'd like to know how that said *twenty-first century*.

As her hand hovered over the telephone, she found herself in a quandary. City Council was going to back the mayor's orders. And Eve knew Connor Sullivan was probably salivating over the prospect of having someone of Matt Brison's caliber handling the final design on behalf of his company. Eve sighed. She also understood family. Matt Brison was trying to make his uncle happy.

Therefore, Eve knew she had only two real choices at this

point—she could either be a gracious loser, or a poor one.

She settled on a combination of the two as her hand dropped onto the desk. She'd counted on this project to help her earn bigger design roles. Instead, she'd be fighting to keep the budget from getting out of control. She'd do it, though. Eve's reputation as a project manager was every bit as important to her as Matt Brison's was to him.

"I guess I should be welcoming you on board, then," she said. "I'll be happy to share some of my ideas with you."

Eve made the offer with no real hope of it being accepted. She shuddered to think what expenses Matt Brison would incur. Architects considered themselves answerable only to God and always ran projects way over budget, leaving Eve holding the bag. Or, rather, a handful of invoices she would then have to justify.

Between the over-qualified architect and his moron uncle, Eve's migraine medication would need to be taken at a double dose.

Chapter Two

Eve unclenched her fingers and took a deep breath. At least she controlled the purse-strings, and therefore, much of the project. That thought raised her flagging spirits. She could make an architect stick to a budget; she'd done it before. This architect was no different than any other she'd worked with.

Except this one was famous. And the mayor's nephew.

She rubbed her aching temple.

"I'd love to see your ideas," Matt said, his words catching her by surprise. "May I?"

Before she had time to recover, he'd flicked on a desk lamp and was standing in front of her drafting table, gazing down at house plans she'd finished a few nights ago for a private client. She'd picked them up from the printer on her way to work that morning so she could give them one last proof before dropping them off.

The irony of the situation did not escape her. She had just been criticizing one of the country's finest young architects, yet his first sample of her own work—other than the plans he claimed to have reviewed—was to be the house plans for a client who could give Bob Anderson a run for his money.

She forced herself to move in a calm and assured manner

when what she really wanted to do was dive across her desk and throw her body over those plans to hide them from sight. "Those are for a client who is very particular about what he wants."

Matt stared at the plans, his expression noncommittal. The expensive Italian suit made her self-conscious about her own worn-out, shiny-kneed jeans, and she couldn't remember if she'd put on any makeup that morning. When she worked on site, regulations required her to wear steel-toed boots and a hard hat. They said nothing about lipstick. She wished they were having this conversation in her office at Sullivan Construction, and she were wearing her high heels.

Chewing on her naked lower lip, Eve tried not to notice how very tall he was or how very blue those eyes were when he looked at her. She tried not to notice the beginnings of a five o'clock shadow on a strong jaw or that he had a slight cleft at the curve of his mouth. She also tried not to notice how her breath quickened when his arm brushed against her shoulder.

She was unsuccessful on all counts.

He ran a hand through his short-cropped black hair and glanced down at her. His eyes twinkled with a glimmer of sympathy. Pure, physical attraction struck her, hard.

"I've had difficult clients, too. Tell you what," he continued. "Why don't we schedule a meeting to share our ideas? That will give me time to get some sketches together to show you."

Time to prepare would be good, although she was was too rattled to make a firm commitment. "I have a lot of work on the go right now, but I should be available early next week."

They were still in front of the drafting table, standing too close together. Matt was making no signs of leaving, just watching her face, and Eve wasn't sure what to do about it.

"I wouldn't mind having a quick tour of this site," he

hinted, his incredible eyes crinkling at the corners.

While she was cautious of his motives, Eve wasn't about to pass up a chance to wow him with her accomplishments. She'd seen his work; let him see hers. "I'll get you a hard hat."

She grabbed her own, as well as a spare kept on a hook on the wall for visitors. She passed the spare to Matt. As he took it, his fingers caught hers, just their tips brushing the backs of her knuckles, and when she looked up at him, he smiled into her eyes. "Thanks."

The fine dark shadow on his jaw showed off the perfect whiteness of his teeth. Eve blinked. The man was gorgeous. And he knew how to rock it.

She put more distance between them and settled her hat in place. She reached for the door, but Matt got to it first. She couldn't remember the last time someone had held a door for her out of politeness and not because her hands were full.

He got full marks for manners. The jury was still out on his intentions.

They both stepped from the dingy trailer into the sunshine. Shouting to the site supervisor to let him know where she was going, she led Matt across the torn-up lot to the heavy, steel doors of the new federal building.

Inside, black mirrors greeted them from an otherwise empty foyer. Thick cables crisscrossed the dusty granite floors. The smell of drying paint from the glassed-in office suites tickled her nose, while clouds of Gyprock dust drifted in the air. Hammers thundered in far-off parts of the building.

Eve loved everything about a construction site, including the creative challenge of working within a budget. Here, outer offices were given extra attention while inner offices were designed more for function to save money. Nowhere, however, had corners been cut.

She was proud of this particular project and, as she

walked him through, didn't try to hide it. She'd done this design, too. She knew just where she could cut costs—and those cuts usually involved the little details most architects considered important to their professional identities. What would an architect of Matt's caliber do when she had to tell him he couldn't have some of those pricy little details?

"Nice," he said when they were back in the foyer, his expression warm and unsettling.

Eve tried not to feel insulted by his lack of enthusiasm. It wasn't the Taj Mahal, granted, but he could at least acknowledge it for what it was: a quality piece of construction.

Then she wondered if it was the building he thought was nice or if he meant something else. She recalled the twinkle in his eye earlier. She knew how to deal with it when men were blatantly interested in her. She could laugh it off and pretend they were joking, and no one was offended. But Matt was subtler than that. More charming.

And Eve was uncomfortable with this kind of attention. She had no idea how to respond.

"What would you have done differently?" she asked.

As Matt looked around, he appeared to be giving the question careful consideration. Then those blue eyes fixed back on her. Twin creases embracing the corners of his mouth made a brief, attention-grabbing appearance. "For starters, I'd have added a Starbucks."

Eve wanted to laugh, but she wasn't sure he'd meant to be funny. He was too hard to read, so she left it alone.

He walked with her back to the trailer, and the site supervisor came over to greet them. Eve introduced the two men, then she excused herself with a lame comment about mountains of paperwork to be done.

She dashed back into her office, leaving them to talk outside in the sunshine. Instead of digging into the invoices, however, she peered through a crack in the blinds and waited for Matt to leave.

She didn't want to find Bob Anderson's interloping, over-priced nephew reasonable, understanding, or most especially, attractive. She didn't want to see the sympathy, or the interest, or even the humor, in his eyes. She'd fallen for his type before, and it had been a disaster.

She breathed a little easier once he was gone, then told herself to relax. She was being ridiculous. He was showing professional courtesy, nothing more. As long as he didn't interfere with her doing her job, there was nothing for her to worry about.

She slumped back in her chair. Who was she trying to kid? She had yet to meet an architect who didn't interfere with her job.

The phone rang, and Eve wished she could ignore it and stick her head under something dark and heavy. Instead, she answered it. "Hello?"

"Hello, Eve."

Just what she needed. A phone call from her mother.

A selfish thought lifted her spirits. Maybe her parents' fortieth anniversary party was about to be canceled.

No such luck.

"I'm planning the menu for the party," her mother said. "I thought I'd make tourtière, just for you. You *will* be coming, won't you?"

There it was again—the guilt trip. The anxious little quiver to her mother's voice, making it sound as if the anniversary would be a disaster if Eve wasn't there. In fairness, their large, Acadian French family was very close-knit, and they'd all be disappointed if she didn't show up.

"I wouldn't miss it," Eve said, smothering her sigh. After all, why wouldn't she want to hear tired family jokes about her oddball career choice, her failed marriage, and, oh yes, the current lack of a man in her life?

They might be a close family, but that didn't always translate into understanding and sensitivity.

She made the appropriate noises as her mother outlined the family weekend she'd planned. Then Eve said she had work to do and extricated herself from what would surely be a much longer conversation than she wanted to deal with just then.

The second Eve said good-bye and hung up, however, the phone rang again. She made a face at it. What detail could her mother possibly have forgotten?

"Have you missed me?" whispered a low, husky, male voice.

Eve hadn't heard that voice in over five years…and had hoped never to hear again.

Chapter Three

"Why do I need an escort for your fundraiser?"

Matt cradled the phone between his shoulder and ear and stood splay-legged at the large window in his hotel room. He'd turned down his uncle's invitation to stay at his house. Uncle Bob was an extrovert who liked to entertain, while Matt preferred peace and quiet. A hotel was definitely the best option.

"You aren't the one in need of an escort," his uncle said over the clatter of caterers Matt could hear working in the background. "I doubt if Eve wants to come so much as her boss wants her here, and Connor Sullivan's kind of old-school. He doesn't think a woman should show up at these things unescorted. I told him you'd be happy to bring her."

His uncle paused, waiting for some response, but Matt said nothing. It had been three days since he'd introduced himself to the pretty little project manager, and as yet she'd made no effort to contact him so they could sit down and talk. That might be because she was the draftsman who'd done the preliminary designs—an important detail he'd found out too late, after he'd already put his big foot in his mouth. What was it he'd said?

City Council has decided they want to hire a professional.

He was well aware of how condescending he must have sounded, and when he looked back, he should have noticed that she'd been insulted. She'd gotten very distant and then made no secret of the fact she couldn't wait to be rid of him.

It was never nice to be set aside in favor of someone with higher qualifications, and while he did have his professional brand to consider, he hadn't intended to come across as that guy who bought into his own fame and fortune and dismissed any input from others.

Or he might have come on a little too strong after she'd made it plain she wasn't interested. But he'd been intrigued, and possibly challenged, by her complete lack of interest, both in his work and in him.

Somehow, he didn't think she'd find an arranged date with him a whole lot of fun.

"Come on, Mattie," his uncle wheedled. "I'm not asking you to marry her. Just spend a few hours with her. It won't kill you. Besides, you both have common interests. You'll be working together. And I bet she looks half decent in a dress."

Matt had no doubt she would, but he had other reservations regarding the pint-sized woman with the hot-chocolate eyes and tempting lips. Being asked at the last minute to escort her to a fundraising reception at his uncle's home did nothing to ease them. Maybe it was because his uncle was trying too hard to sound casual. That usually meant he was up to no good.

Matt stared out at the city lights sparkling across the black waters of the harbor. Several moored ships glowed against the dusky skyline, their masts decked out like great, white Christmas trees for the hordes of tourists swarming the waterfront.

"I have work to do," he told his uncle. "Just because

I'm not in my office doesn't mean I can let things pile up." A thought landed and took root. "You aren't trying to hook us up, are you?"

"You and *Eve*? Don't even joke about such a thing. I'm not getting any younger, and my heart won't take it." His uncle sounded so entertained by the idea that Matt's suspicions were eased. Whatever his uncle was up to, matchmaking wasn't it. "But I need you here tonight, and it won't hurt to make Connor happy." Uncle Bob lowered his voice, as if about to convey a big secret he didn't want anyone to overhear.

A reluctant grin tugged at Matt's lips. Oh yeah. Those caterers were probably dying to find out what his uncle's current scheme was. And he knew his uncle. There had to be one.

"There are a few councilors I want you to talk to," Bob admitted. "They aren't convinced yet about the need for design changes, and I'm hoping you can sway them."

So that was what his uncle was up to. Matt relaxed. Business, he could understand. And family loyalty. Uncle Bob might not be keeping score but Matt was, and Matt owed him for all the years he'd tried his best to fill in as a father. If Uncle Bob wanted a modern City Hall, then that was what he'd get. Matt could impress a few councilors.

It was the unimpressed project manager he seemed to be having the difficulty with. He wondered what her type was. And why he wasn't it.

Maybe he'd find out at the fundraiser. He might even get a chance to make amends.

"Okay," he said, feeling more enthusiastic than he had a few minutes ago. "What time should I be there?"

"Eve will pick you up around eight."

Matt disconnected and tossed his phone into a padded armchair, then rubbed his stubbly chin. He glanced at his watch. Plenty of time for a shower and shave.

...

Eve hopped around her bedroom on one foot, trying to stuff the other into an uncooperative pair of pantyhose while cursing the man who'd invented them. Then, she cursed men in general.

I forgive you, Eve, Claude, her ex-husband, had said.

Even after three days, her anger over that statement hadn't burned itself out. It seemed they had vastly different recollections as to why their two-week marriage had ended, and she didn't feel quite as forgiving about them as Claude. Maybe she should have said so before blowing that rape whistle in his ear.

To call her five years later to tell her he forgave her for some figment of his imagination was only one example of his unfortunate tendency to fixate.

For what felt like the millionth time, she wondered what it was that had attracted her to him in the first place. Flattery, she supposed. He'd been a marine biologist with a PhD who traveled all over the world, and had been working on a research project in the Bay of Fundy, near her small Acadian hometown, the summer they'd met. Handsome and brilliant, he'd treated her like the sun rose and set for her pleasure alone. He was handsome, too, in a bookish, nerdy kind of way. The attention had been overwhelming for a girl who'd seen nothing of the world and never gotten more than a drafting diploma from the local community college.

His teasing about that education should have served as her first warning. It hadn't taken her two days after the wedding to realize the magnitude of her mistake. Claude's adoration turned to obsession in the blink of an eye. He'd trashed their apartment because he hadn't liked her talking to an old boyfriend from high school. He'd called her stupid on several occasions, and she'd almost begun to believe it. After all, she'd made the mistake of marrying him.

But when he said they were going to spend the next few years on an isolated island in the Pacific doing marine research, and had given her only a few days to prepare, Eve dragged herself out of denial and finally balked. He'd actually raised a hand to hit her, violent anger burning in his eyes, and that was the end, as far as she was concerned. An older brother had taught her how to defend herself, and she'd laid Claude out flat, breaking his nose and blackening both of his eyes, then packed her bags and moved home.

When faced with a choice between leaving for the Pacific and pursuing her, Claude had chosen to leave—as she'd expected him to, despite his possessive tendencies. She'd shown herself to not be his puppet anymore.

All she told her family was that she wasn't about to live on a deserted island that had no electricity or modern medical care. She hadn't said a word about Claude; Eve had her pride.

Once she was sure Claude was out of the country, she'd moved to Halifax and talked her way into the construction business. She'd started off with only private clients before hiring on with Sullivan Construction and scraping her way up the ladder to project manager. She'd worked long and hard to get where she was.

And now, Claude was back. She'd never really known him, she now understood. She had no idea if he'd try to contact her again, or what his motives were for doing so in the first place. He'd signed the divorce papers years ago, and she'd assumed they were through. That rape whistle she'd blown in his ear should have been enough to convince him, the arrogant bastard.

She finished wriggling into her uncooperative pantyhose and zipped into her dress, checking the clock by her bed. She had to go pick up her "date" soon.

Eve smoothed her dress and stood up taller. If there was one important lesson she'd learned from the whole experience with Claude—and with her job—it was not to get involved with clever, ambitious, overly confident men. Not professionally, and definitely not personally. They were good at hiding their true natures behind a thin layer of charm.

And Matt Brison was charming.

He might be an architect, not a biologist, but brilliant was brilliant. The ego was there. The sense of self-entitlement. Deep down, on the level that mattered, he made Eve uneasy.

So why she'd agreed to accompany him to the fundraiser tonight she would never know, although it likely had a lot to do with her paycheck. If she wanted to remain on the City Hall project, Connor Sullivan had hinted, she'd better paste on a smile and pretend to be pleased.

She grabbed her shoes and her purse and sprinted down the stairs.

...

It was ten minutes past eight by the time she parked in the hotel's gloomy, underground parking garage.

She examined her makeup in the rearview mirror one last time before climbing out of the car and hitching down the tight skirt of her black dress. She wished she'd had something more conservative to wear than a dress her brothers had given her as a joke for her twenty-ninth birthday. They said it was to help her catch a man before she became an old woman of thirty.

She'd rather catch a bad cold.

The dank smell of sweating cement and automobile fumes ambushed her as she tottered to the elevators. The sound of her high heels tapping on concrete echoed eerily throughout the empty parking garage. Eve tried not to think about the long shadows and dark corners created by the inadequate overhead lighting, and breathed a small sigh of relief when the elevator doors slid closed behind her.

There was no doubt about it. The phone call from Claude had left her nervous and on edge, and that just made her angrier. If she got to pick her next life, she was coming back as a man. A huge, hairy one.

The elevator doors hummed open. She stepped into the hotel lobby, crossed to the front desk, and asked the clerk to call Matt's room to let him know his ride was waiting. She reminded herself she was a professional and to act like one, then caught a glimpse of herself in a mirror and had an uneasy addendum to that thought.

Did this dress make her look like the wrong kind of professional?

Matt's gaze wandered around the lobby, then lingered appreciatively on the mirrored reflection of a woman standing near one of the potted plants.

Recognition snagged his insides. It couldn't be.

The thick mass of auburn hair was now twisted in a smooth knot and pinned at her crown. A light touch of makeup emphasized large eyes and long, dark lashes, and her plump lips demanded his attention. She wore a black dress that clung to her curves. The dress fit her perfectly, granted, but it showed a lot of leg—and she had great legs.

Matt's mouth went dry. Somehow he doubted those high

heels had steel toes.

She watched him approach with an air of hesitation about her that disarmed him even more.

She held out a hand to greet him. That handshake put them right back on a professional footing and reminded him she hadn't planned the evening for his entertainment. This was business, not pleasure.

"I'm sorry I'm late," she said.

"Not a problem," he managed to reply, despite the wad of cotton coating his tongue. "You look very lovely."

"Thank you."

Tough audience. He might have been commenting on the weather for all the reaction the compliment got from her. He usually didn't have to work this hard to give a woman a reason to like him.

Surely he could find some way to redeem himself for his poor first impression.

They walked together to the elevator, noticing again how very small she was in spite of her towering heels. And how much more reserved she seemed than she'd been on site. He thought maybe he preferred her in work boots. At least then he'd had something to say to her.

Although, up until now, he'd said all the wrong things. He wondered how he could lead up to an apology without coming off sounding like a condescending ass again.

He punched the button beside the gleaming, silver elevator doors. The doors slid open, and they stepped inside.

"Out of curiosity," he said. "What kind of toys did you play with when you were a little girl?"

Her lovely eyes were puzzled as she glanced up at him through those thick lashes. The elevator gave a slight jerk, and Matt took her elbow to steady her, her skin surprisingly soft and smooth beneath his touch.

"The usual girl stuff, I guess. My mother had a thing about buying me dolls." Eve's button nose crinkled, and she looked amused—and maybe a little embarrassed. "But my favorite was a dump truck one of my brothers abandoned. Why?"

Matt felt a flash of relief. That sounded more like what he'd expected. And a great deal more interesting. "Just curious."

He remembered to release her elbow, then didn't know what to do with his hand so he stuck it in his pocket. When they reached the parking level, he followed her to her car.

He frowned as he looked around the deserted garage. "You shouldn't park down here. It's not safe."

She reached into her glittery evening bag for the keys. "I grew up with three older brothers." She pressed a button and unlocked the doors. "I can take care of myself."

Matt waited until she'd slid into the driver's side before getting in himself, then turned to face her, propping his elbow on the back of the seat. "Having three brothers isn't much help if you're alone when you're mugged." Or worse.

She inserted the key in the ignition, and the engine turned over as she gave a little shrug. "It is when one of them teaches self-defense courses and makes you practice."

She backed the car out of the parking space with the skill of a stock-car racer, then, with a heavy foot on the gas, shot out of the garage and into the street.

Matt yanked the seatbelt across his chest and hips and clicked it into place. He ran his fingertips over the dash. "Does this car have a passenger-side air bag?"

Eve's supple lips curved. Slowing down to navigate a sharp corner, she turned onto a quiet street and headed for the south end of the city.

"I'm really a very good driver," she assured him. "I've never had an accident." She peered at him again, and Matt found himself holding his breath when her smile deepened.

"Mind you, I've only had my license for three weeks."

His jaw started to drop and then he snapped it shut. "That's a joke, right?"

"Good heavens. Lighten up a little. Of course, it's a joke. I—"

Something on the sidewalk caught her attention. She muttered an exclamation and slammed on the brakes, throwing them both forward against their locked seatbelts. Matt grabbed for the dash with both hands, then looked over to make sure she was okay.

"Sorry," she said. "I thought I saw someone I knew."

If so, then it wasn't a person she liked. Her hand trembled slightly on the gearshift, and it took her a moment to get the car back in motion, but it was the expression on her face that struck Matt the most. Her eyes darted back and forth like she was scanning the terrain for enemy snipers. She looked almost…

Hunted was the word that sprang to mind.

Eve hoped she had lipstick on her teeth. The way Matt had stared at her during the rest of the drive meant it was either that, or he thought she was crazy.

She paused in the doorway of the large reception room and gave her front teeth a quick, furtive buff with her thumb just to be safe. Nope. No lipstick. He thought she was crazy.

She didn't blame him. She wanted to get this evening over with as quickly as possible. She wasn't in the mood for dodging budget questions on a design that didn't exist, and diplomacy wasn't one of her strengths. Neither did she care for this type of function. She didn't golf, she didn't sail, and she didn't have a million dollars to give away to some worthy cause.

But Matt looked all male-model gorgeous in a charcoal-gray suit that had to have been custom-made for him. He fit right in. This was his world, not hers.

He gestured for her to precede him through the doorway, and when she took a step forward, he placed a hand on the small of her back. His thumb subtly skimmed the swell of her hip. Eve wrestled a spontaneous, bone-melting desire to arch against his touch like a cat at a scratching post, then almost had a panic attack. She edged away from his lingering hand, aware she was overreacting to what amounted to nothing more than a gentlemanly gesture.

Matt grabbed them a glass of wine from a passing waiter as a smiling middle-aged woman in her forties, with artificial blond hair and an ill-fitting dress, jiggled her matronly body in their direction. Eve, glad for the diversion, scanned her memory, trying to come up with a name. Marion Something-or-other. Provincial Government, Department of Tourism and Culture.

Her stomach let out a little flutter of excitement. Eve had been trying for months to get work with these people. They had a few restoration projects that she'd love to be involved in.

The older woman extended a heavily ringed hand. "Hello, Ms. Doucette. I was hoping I might see you here this evening. We've never been formally introduced. I'm Marion Balcom." Her gaze swept over to include Matt. "And you must be Matt Brison," she said, shaking hands with him, too, before zeroing back in on Eve. "It's amazing how fast Bob made all this happen, isn't it? There hasn't been much press coverage on this whole project, yet already Culture and Tourism has been fielding calls from the Historical Society regarding what will happen to the current City Hall building."

"I'm the project manager," Eve explained, her head still

foggy from the touch of Matt's hand. She took a sip of her drink. "I'm in charge of the expenditures and cost analyses, so that's not really my area, but it's my understanding that the old Hall has been slated for decommission."

"Then the old Hall isn't worth saving?"

Eve was no good at figuring out what information people were really trying to get from her, and it was obvious Marion wanted something. For Eve's part, she wanted to make a good impression.

"That depends on how much money you're willing to spend on it," she replied carefully. "According to the engineer's report the answer is yes, it can be saved, but if the building is to be decommissioned, then my guess would be the city can't afford the expense of renovating. Sometimes it's cheaper to start from scratch."

"Hmm." Marion's eyes again rested on Matt, who'd been quietly listening. "Mr. Brison, I thought your designs tended to be much more sophisticated than anything our quiet little city would require. Hadn't other plans already been approved?"

Again, Eve wondered where Marion was headed with her questioning. She was on the prowl for something, though.

"This is a design/build project," Matt explained. "The preliminary blueprints are used as a guideline so the general contractor can provide cost estimates and a timeline for completion. I'll be the one making sure the client gets what they really want for the final design."

His eyes went to Eve on that last comment, as if he were trying to get her concurrence. Well, he wasn't going to get it. Clearly, he needed a reminder that technically, in this instance, he worked for the general contractor and not the client — and there was a difference between what the client might want and what the client could afford. Architects tended to forget funny little details like that.

She opened her mouth to speak as their host wove his way through the crowd toward them. Tall, with a thick shock of silver hair and blue eyes much the same color as his nephew's, Bob's face was a wreath of smiles.

Eve clenched her teeth. The last time he'd smiled at her like that, she'd found herself working pro bono. And the thing about free labor was that one tended to get what one paid for.

Which reminded her, she still had some doors to shave down and hang at that Internet café. The other volunteers didn't know how, and the bathroom doors had to be installed for the café to pass a building inspection.

"Hey, Matt. Evie." Bob pumped her hand. "You look absolutely beautiful this evening. Glad you could make it. By the way, thanks for picking Matt up." His voice carried, and a few people laughed. Even Marion smiled.

Eve's cheeks stung with heat. "The hotel was on my way," she said, willing him to spontaneously combust. The twitch of a muscle under Matt's jaw indicated he was trying to control a grin of his own.

"I see my husband's hooked up with a colleague," Marion said, excusing herself. "Never leave two healthcare specialists from the same research study alone at a party. They'll be talking about infectious diseases all evening if I don't go put a stop to it."

"We'll find time to chat later," Bob said to her. He shifted his drink to his other hand and turned back to Eve.

Her fingers curled around her wineglass. She vowed she was not going to let him talk her into anything, but he had a way of getting what he wanted that was truly astounding. In a previous lifetime, he'd no doubt sold snake oil to unsuspecting settlers.

"Be honest," Bob said as he clapped a hand to his nephew's shoulder. "Now that you've met him, you have to agree that getting Mattie to do the design for City Hall is a real coup. He'll set a precedent for modernizing this city, and before you know it, we'll be on the international map."

Matt lifted his eyebrows. *Well?* His amused look challenged her. *Am I a coup or what?*

"We're already on the international map," Eve said, trying to ignore Matt's efforts to make her smile back at him. It was no easy feat—that was one killer smile he possessed.

"We have one of the largest and deepest natural harbors along the Eastern seaboard. And for the record," she added, "I don't think the city needs to be modernized. More and more historic sites are being lost to glass and steel projects with no character. Glass and steel certainly have their place, but if we don't protect our downtown district, it will no longer have the atmosphere that makes it such an attraction to tourists and movie companies."

Bob gave a low chuckle, as if she'd said something cute. Eve had the horrible fear he was about to pat her on the head. If he did, she'd be forced to lay him out flat at his own reception. She tolerated him calling her *Evie*, but she had boundaries.

"Sweetheart, there's more to attracting tourism and movie companies to the downtown core than a few old buildings."

Eve refocused the conversation. "What about the budget?" she asked. "Sullivan Construction has already won the contract. Technically Matt works for us now, and our budget dictates his plans will have to be a bit more practical than he's used to."

"Excuse me for interrupting, but my plans are always practical." Matt's deceptively soft voice rumbled above her head, enveloping Eve's insides in a sudden flash of heat. He had a voice like polished oak. Solid, but smooth. "Every inch of space is both usable and aesthetic."

"But can you make sure it's affordable, too?" she challenged, determined not to forget where her loyalties lay.

"That's what I like about you, Evie." Bob nodded a greeting to a cadaverous man in a dark suit walking by. "You're so passionate when it comes to money. Has anyone ever told you that you worry too much?"

Eve set her untouched drink on a nearby table, the blood pounding in her temples like the low, slow throbbing of a drum. She'd show him just how passionate she could be when the necessity arose. She was tired of Bob not taking her seriously. "I get paid to worry about budget money."

"Uncle Bob." Matt's firm hand took possession of Eve's punching arm. "Do you mind if I borrow Eve for a few moments?"

"Not at all," Bob said, already scanning the room like a shark sniffing out blood in the water. "You kids go have fun."

Matt hustled her down a short hall, through an open set of sliding glass doors, and onto a small flagstone patio cobwebbed in shadows.

"In most circles, it's considered impolite to punch your host in the nose," he said, once they were outside. He sounded amused, but it was hard for Eve to tell in the dark.

"I wasn't going to punch Bob," she protested, ninety-nine percent certain she was telling the truth. "I was only going to give him my opinion."

"That can be just as bloody, sometimes. I thought you might want to think about it for a few moments." He released her arm as if reluctant to do so, his fingers lingering long enough to make Eve's mouth go dry. "If you still want to give him your opinion after that, hey, I'll even hold him down for you."

"Bob could use a good opinion every once in a while." Eve pinched the bridge of her nose. "I don't know why I let him get to me," she nearly growled.

"I'm sure he gets to a lot of people," Matt said.

"Now there's an understatement."

Eve dropped onto one of the stone benches, the sweet scent from a mock orange bush drifting on the fresh evening air that whispered over her bare skin. Light streamed through large windows, bathing a section of the small patio in a gentle glow. A leafy grape arbor hid them from sight if anyone should happen to glance outside. Matt settled beside her, stretching out his long legs. She leaned forward and propped her chin on her hand, then tilted her head sideways to look up at him. A jolt of awareness tightened her chest in a way that was hard to ignore, but Eve tried her best. She doubted they shared the same sense of humor. He was far from spontaneous. She suspected he was more than a little uptight, in fact.

And they were colleagues. She wasn't planning to let attraction overrule common sense, not when it came to her work, but being friendly would get her more cooperation than acting crazy. Matt wasn't to blame for the things his uncle said or did. Or what Claude had done, either.

"Since we're going to be working together, there's something you should know about me. I have a quick temper," she said.

He clapped a hand over his heart. "I would never have guessed."

That made her laugh. "Hard to believe, isn't it?"

The last of her anger wafted away. She shouldn't let Bob's cavalier attitude irritate her so much. She was, indeed, passionate about her work, and these days, it was all the passion she seemed to possess. She wiggled her toes inside her narrow shoes, keenly aware of the male presence beside her. She couldn't remember the last time she'd been alone in the dark with a man, and just like that, Eve realized the dangerous position she'd put herself in. She wasn't ready for another man in her life.

And this was most definitely the wrong man for her even if she were. Matt was a rich and famous architect. She'd be nothing more than entertainment to someone like him. She had more self-respect than that, and she'd earned it the hard way.

She eased away from him so that they weren't sitting so close.

"Uncle Bob's not so bad once you get to know him," Matt said.

Eve had known Bob for three years, and so far, she hadn't seen any real improvement. He could be charming, yes, but he never did anything without a motive. Quite frankly, he made her head tired.

"Why did he insist Sullivan Construction hire you, anyway?" she asked. She couldn't see what would be in this for Matt. He certainly wasn't doing it for the glory. Or the money. "You must have more important projects you could be working on."

"Yes, but this project is important to my uncle." Eve could feel the affection in his smooth voice. In fact, she felt it all the way to her toes. "He's been good to my mother and me. I'm grateful to be given the opportunity to do something for him in return."

She couldn't argue with that. "But you're working for the contractor," Eve felt compelled to remind him.

Matt studied the tips of his shoes with casual disinterest. "So I've heard."

"And I control the budget."

"I keep hearing that, too."

"Since those two things are true," she persisted, "your design will have to meet with my approval before it goes to the client."

Matt tapped the fingers of one hand against his pant leg. He turned his attention from the tips of his shoes to her face.

"Why didn't you just come right out and tell me that you did the preliminary design when I introduced myself?" he asked.

The question caught her off guard. Someone must have told him.

"That's not what this is about," she said.

"I think it is." His fingers ceased their tapping. "There was nothing wrong with your design, Eve. It was good. But the truth is, the client wants something different." He blew out a sigh. "We both know that the one with the final say on the new design will be the architect. That happens to be me. So, why don't you tell me what your real objection to working with me is?"

He paused a beat. Heat entered his unwavering gaze. He edged closer, filling the small space she'd created between them.

"Because I'm starting to think that it's personal."

Chapter Four

He had hoped to get a chance to apologize to her this evening for dismissing her design. Instead, he'd ended up pointing out, once again, how his professional designation trumped hers.

But he did think this was personal, and he couldn't quite put his finger on why. Aside from that one little blunder, he'd been nothing but friendly. Maybe she was transferring her annoyance with his uncle—and yes, he knew Uncle Bob could be annoying—onto him.

Sounds from the gathering inside drifted around them in the moonlight as he waited for her reaction.

"I don't even know you," Eve said. "But I know your work. Even if the city does want to hire a *professional*, I think you have to agree that you're the wrong one for this job." She stood and smoothed silky fabric down over her slim hips. "Excuse me. I need another drink."

"Not so fast." Matt caught her hand before she could walk away. He, too, rose to his feet, then had to dip his head in order to see her face as she looked away. "This is a small project in an even smaller town. If it's not personal, and we're going to be working together for the next few months, then it might as well be on friendly terms. I still want to see your ideas."

She eased her fingers from his grasp. "This might be a small project to you, but to me, it's important. But don't worry. You won't need to do me any favors. I have my own reputation in this city. Small as it is."

He had handled this badly. All her contradictions, and passion for her work, intrigued him. But he still thought there was more to her objection to him than a dislike for his work.

"I'm not doing you a favor," he said. "I'm always open to ideas."

"Thanks. I appreciate the opportunity. It's very generous of you."

The words were polite but hardly brimming with enthusiasm. Matt tried not to grin. At least she wasn't going to be stroking his ego, which was kind of refreshing. Not to mention, challenging.

She turned to the patio doors, paused as if about to say something more, then peered through a crack in the sheer curtains.

"Oh, nuts. Here comes Connor's wife, Lena," she whispered. "The last time she caught me at one of these functions, I spent two hours listening to her talk about the horrors of breastfeeding and the agony of having an older husband who doesn't pay enough attention to her. If you really want to do me a favor, tell her you haven't seen me."

With that, Eve climbed over one of the stone benches and ducked behind a low cedar hedge.

Matt's mouth dropped open.

The glass doors slid back and an elegant, black-haired Latina woman stepped onto the flagstones. He vaguely recalled having been introduced to her at some point in time.

"Excuse me," she said. "I thought I saw Eve come out here."

There was a hint of a question to her fluid, heavily accented words that should have warned him, but Matt's attention was focused elsewhere. His eyes darted to the bushes, unsure of the proper protocol for this type of scenario.

"Eve went to powder her nose," he said, feeling like an idiot. Then his sense of humor took over. "But she should be back any moment. You're welcome to wait with me if you'd like."

The bushes behind him rustled at that. He was beginning to enjoy this—but just a little.

"I would like that very much." Lena Sullivan moved a little closer—too close—and it suddenly occurred to Matt that the situation was potentially even more awkward than he'd first thought. He hoped he'd mistaken the delight in her tone. "I have been wanting to catch you alone from the moment I saw you."

Nope. It seemed he hadn't mistaken anything.

"Oh?" Matt didn't know what else to say. Was Eve hearing any of this? If so, she could at least have the decency to help him out.

Lena moved closer still. "Yes." She placed a hand on his chest, and he swallowed, hard. "I would imagine you and I have a lot in common."

He did his best to sound discouraging. "Really?"

Light fingers began to draw circles on his shirtfront. "You are alone in a strange city, and no doubt lonely. I am alone in a strange country where nobody understands me." Lena's voice trembled. "And I am *definitely* lonely."

Matt's mind raced. The woman was hitting on him, and he had to do something to make her stop. This was a prime reason why he most definitely wasn't looking for a trophy wife. That was the trouble with trophies—sooner or later, they landed with the competition.

"Eve should be back any moment," he repeated, inching backward. "She's a jealous woman, Lena. I'd hate to have her misinterpret the fact that you and I are out here alone together."

Lena's hands dropped to her sides, much to his relief. Her accent grew more pronounced, although he suspected that was an affectation. Most men likely found it charming.

"I had no idea you were a couple. Eve, she does not normally bother with the men."

"No?" That was nice to know…although Eve probably didn't bother with men because she scared them off.

"I thought this was a business event," Lena added. "Connor sometimes asks her to introduce the V-I-Ps around on behalf of the company."

"It's definitely not strictly business between me and Eve," he said.

Lena heaved her impressive breasts. "I would hate to get you into trouble with her." She gave his tie a little tug. "Maybe I will see you later?"

She sauntered off with an elegant sway to her hips and a smoldering glance over her shoulder. Matt waited until he was certain she was gone before crossing to the bench Eve had hurdled.

"Get back up here," he grumbled, scanning the long shadows. "I want to talk to you."

Eve's voice came from out of the darkness. "I'd be angry with you," she said with an air of satisfaction, "except you got exactly what you deserved. 'You're welcome to wait with me if you'd like,'" she parroted, then mumbled something that sounded suspiciously like, "Lena can't resist the good-looking ones."

At least she thought he was good-looking. That meant one thing had gone right so far this evening.

"You could have warned me about her *before* you did your disappearing act," Matt said. He placed one knee on the bench and peered into the bushes. "Would you get up here where I can see you?"

The bushes rustled again. "I can't."

Matt wondered how long they had before someone else wandered outside and found them like this. He was torn between fascination and maintaining his dignity. She didn't seem all that concerned about hers.

"What do you mean, you can't?"

"I mean," Eve explained in a matter-of-fact tone, "that my dress is snagged on a twig, and I'm trying to get it free without tearing anything."

"Let me give you a hand." Leaning over the bench in the direction of her voice, he parted the bushes and could just make out Eve's form in the darkness. The bushes lurched as she tugged at her dress.

"Don't do that," he warned, stretching out a hand, his fingertips brushing against the fabric. He leaned a little farther, trying to get a grip. "You're going to make things worse. I think I can get it if I just—"

He moved forward one inch too far and tumbled headfirst into his uncle's fragrant shrubbery. Matt rolled, spit out a mouthful of dirt, and spared a fleeting thought for the kind of mulch his uncle's gardener might use. Whatever it was, he hoped a dry cleaner could get the smell off his suit.

Then, Eve burst into soft peals of laughter that made him forget all about Lena, the crowd, the threat of discovery, and even the prickly underbrush jabbing through his clothing.

She had the most incredible laugh. It wasn't a polite little party laugh, either, the kind he was used to hearing from women. It came from deep inside her, too big for her tiny frame, like she'd explode if she didn't let it out. It invited anyone who heard it to laugh along with her, and Matt felt every inch of his body respond to it.

She didn't seem to care that her dress was most likely ruined or that her hair was a mess. And it was obvious she hadn't given any thought as to how they were going to explain this to any of the other people present. Matt couldn't help but be charmed, and maybe a little bit envious. Everything she did, she did with passion—he could tell that about her already. What would it be like to live life like that?

That was when the situation really struck him. He was rolling around in his uncle's shrubbery with a sexy new colleague in a peekaboo dress. A company code of ethics didn't quite have this one covered. He wasn't too sure what to do about it—or when he'd become such an old man.

Because personally, he didn't see how it would do any real harm.

The night was warm, and the air was heavy with the threat of approaching rain. If they didn't move soon they'd be mud wrestling, too.

Still, he was no longer in any hurry to go anywhere. No one could see them even if they did come out on the patio. He figured this put them well past the first base of any relationship, professional or otherwise, and wondered if it would be inappropriate to kiss her.

"You're in luck," he said. "Here's your chance to get to know me better."

"I already know you suck at making excuses." Laughter lingered in her voice. She caught his ribs with an elbow. "Who says 'powder your nose' anymore? What are you, ninety?"

"I panicked. Besides, there may be snow on the roof, but there's plenty of fire in the furnace." He edged closer. "Don't move. I'll unhook your dress."

He pinned her down with the weight of one leg and

reached across her, taking his time, enjoying the moment. She smelled a lot better than the mulch.

The moment stretched. Inside the house, he could hear muted conversation and the faint clatter of plates and glasses.

"We're flattening your uncle's forsythia," Eve said.

"Consider it his punch in the nose."

He finally got a finger under the piece of fabric on the prickly shrub, lifted it, and she was free. Again, he debated the wisdom of kissing her. Something pulled him to her like a magnet. He lowered his hand and ran a thumb across her lower lip.

She froze.

Not the reaction he'd been hoping for.

"I think my dress is untangled now," she said, all the laughter gone, sounding uncertain in a way that only made him want to kiss her more, but for different reasons.

Disappointment mingled with temptation as Matt told himself to be a gentleman. She had hesitated. That meant the fun and games were over.

The sudden swish of the patio doors warned him they were no longer alone. Time dragged to a standstill. Then his uncle's voice boomed from above.

"Mattie? You out here?"

The situation could still be saved as long as his uncle didn't hear them. Matt leaned over, intending to whisper in her ear for Eve to be quiet, but in the process, accidentally pinched the soft flesh of her underarm beneath his elbow.

"Ouch!" she gasped, then clapped a hand to her mouth.

Matt, with an impending sense of doom, dropped his forehead to hers. It seemed there was a downside to a passionate lifestyle.

The outdoor floodlights flared, and the entire area lit up like an operating room. There was an awkward moment of silence.

"It's a big house," his uncle said slowly. "Couldn't you two find a room?"

...

Eve's fingers tightened on the steering wheel as her car hummed along the dark, empty streets. Her hair was a wreck, and Matt's suit was covered in mulch. She had to give Bob credit for handling the situation well. He'd offered to tell people that Matt had been called away on business, giving them time to slink around the side of the house and slither off into the night.

Eve slouched deeper in her seat. There must be a perverse little part of her subconscious that liked to see her humiliate herself. She'd really thought Matt was going to kiss her, and she'd panicked. That suggested it had been either way too long since she'd been kissed by a man, or not long enough. She wasn't sure which.

Or maybe it was because that one phone call from Claude had set her confidence back a few years.

She made a mental note not to be so hard on the men at work the next time they whistled at women. After Lena's performance—and her own—it was apparent that men weren't the only ones who could make idiots of themselves over the opposite sex.

She wished Matt would say something now. Anything. He hadn't spoken a word since they'd reached the car. It was the one punishment in life she found difficult to bear—the silent treatment.

"Look at us," she said brightly, needing to break a silence that felt far too oppressive. "All dressed up, and no place to go."

He grunted, his eyes glued on the road ahead.

"You have a leaf in your hair," she ventured, ignoring the bird's nest in her own.

He cranked open the window, plucked the offending leaf from his hair, and released it into the night.

"I'm sorry," she tried again, willing to start the apologies rolling. "I should never have dodged Lena like that."

"That wasn't your finest moment," he said.

The old, familiar anxiety slowly twisted her stomach in knots, and she resented it. Perhaps she could have handled things differently, but it wasn't as if she'd planned for any of it to happen. She hadn't been alone in those bushes.

"At least I covered for us nicely."

"You told my uncle you lost an earring," Matt said.

"Well, I did." Her fingers strayed to her naked lobe. One of her favorites, too. She really needed to stop playing with them.

"That's the second earring you've lost this week. You should consider using staples." He looked directly at her for the first time since they'd crawled from the bushes and limped to the car. "No offense," he continued, "but you come off a little scary sometimes."

Eve slowed for a corner. "What do you mean?"

"You ordered my uncle to trim his hedge."

"It was a ragged-looking."

"Only because you'd crushed it."

"I crushed it?" If they were going to cast stones about crushing things, she still had his hand imprint on one of her breasts.

"Hey," Matt said. "The hedge was yours. I did the forsythia."

"It's nice of you to remember that I wasn't alone."

"Believe me, it's not something I'm likely to forget."

Eve, concentrating on her driving, missed the grin accompanying his words. All she heard was criticism.

Something inside her snapped. "This is so typical." She swerved around a pothole in the street, narrowly missing the rear end of a parked car. "It's always the woman's fault, never the man's."

Matt shifted in his seat, turning toward her. "Wait a second. I never said—"

"You didn't have to say anything. I know what you meant."

"Eve, I think you're being—"

"I know what I'm being," she interrupted again. She was being an idiot. Her nerves had been wound too tight since Claude's phone call, and now she was taking it out on Matt. She knew the whole disaster of an evening was her fault. Why didn't he yell at her and be done with it? Why was he torturing her like this?

His voice gentled. "Stop the car, please."

Eve could see the train wreck coming but was helpless to stop it. If Matt was about to become all sensitive and understanding, she was going to have him killed. She didn't need sympathy right now. She felt tears welling behind her eyes, and that made her furious—with both him and herself. She hated to cry.

She pulled the car over and double-parked in front of a dark restaurant on a quiet street. Grabbing her handbag and holding it up to the dreary glow of a streetlight, Eve whipped out a twenty-dollar bill and slapped it into Matt's palm.

"Maybe you should call yourself a cab," she said.

Matt stared at the money in his hand, his expression unreadable. Then, he carefully placed the money on the dashboard and glanced into the back seat as if looking for something.

"What are you doing?" she snapped.

"Don't you keep tissues in your car? Women always seem to keep tissues everywhere."

Eve rolled her eyes. Why'd he have to be right all the time?

He reached into the back, and just as his fingers closed around the box, a car with flashing red-and-blue lights pulled up behind them. A few moments later, a stocky police officer rapped on Eve's door. When she rolled down the window, he shone a flashlight into the car's interior.

"What seems to be the trouble?" the officer asked.

"Just a little misunderstanding," Matt said.

"A little misunderstanding, huh?"

The officer's light shone in her eyes. Eve plucked the box of tissues from Matt's hand and helped herself, heartily blowing her nose. The light picked up the money on the dash, then the officer flashed the light back on Eve before returning it to Matt's face. "Whatever you're negotiating, do it someplace else. You're double-parked and blocking traffic."

Matt cleared his throat. "The money is for a cab."

The officer's ruddy face creased into a wide grin. "Whatever you say. Have a nice evening."

Eve watched him walk back to his cruiser, then tucked the used tissue in her bag and tossed the box in the backseat. "I'll drive you home."

"You know what?" Matt's voice turned thoughtful. "I think maybe I'd better take that cab."

She watched as he got out of the car, wanting to tell him she was sorry, and that her ex-husband was the one she was angry with, not him. He was more like a civilian casualty.

Matt hesitated, then reached back in and grabbed the twenty off the dash. "I'm a little short on cash." He gave her an exaggerated smile before he turned away from her.

He had a right to be angry, too. She should be relieved this was how he expressed it. Instead, it made her feel awful. There wasn't much left for her to do other than leave him standing in the street, with the red-and-blue police lights pirouetting behind him. She drove off, a spittle of mist dampening her windshield, guilt and mortification eating at her conscience.

By the time she reached her neighborhood, the mist had graduated to streaming black rivers of rain. She wiped the steam off her windshield with the back of her hand, hoping Matt had his cellphone with him. Otherwise, he was going to have a long, wet walk back to his hotel, and she had enough to apologize for already.

The inky eyes of her house gaped at her as she cut the car engine. She groped for the door handle, wishing she'd thought to leave her front light on. Readying her house key, she made a mad dash through the downpour, fumbled with the deadbolt, then slammed the door shut behind her, shaking the water from her hair and face. The clock on the mantle in her living room chimed the hour, chasing a sudden chill up her backbone.

Her house felt…different.

Half turning, Eve noticed a daub of mud on the first step of the stairs leading to the second story. She tried to think of how that mud might have gotten there and couldn't come up with anything comforting.

Someone had been in her house…and she had a good idea who it had been. But she didn't know whether or not he was still there.

With adrenaline warping through her veins at lightning speed, she jerked open the door and fled back through the rain to her car. It wasn't until she was six blocks from her home that she slowed down.

Pulling the car to the curb, she pressed her hot cheek

against the steering wheel and considered her options. She wondered if she should call the police. Again. And be brushed off. Again. She could still hear the officer's calm, reasoning voice that night years ago when she'd made the decision to leave Claude.

"In order to get a peace bond, you'll have to prove the person poses a threat to your safety. If the person obeys the peace bond for a year, though, you won't be able to get it renewed. Are you sure this is the route you want to go?"

She hadn't bothered back then because he was leaving the country. Besides, she had punched him. He hadn't hit her, he'd only threatened, as far as logistics were concerned. And she wasn't going to the police now only to have them tell her that a phone call, a funny feeling, and a few specks of dirt weren't enough by way of evidence to get her a peace bond this time.

She wasn't going to run crying to her brothers, either. It was a little late to be telling them the truth about her marriage. That window of opportunity had closed a long time ago. She did have work boots and a pair of coveralls in her car, though, and plenty of work left to do at that volunteer project Bob had conned her into. She could spend the night shaving those doors down, then go back to her house when daylight came.

And if she worked hard enough, maybe she could forget for a while that she owed Matt an apology.

...

Matt's long legs ate up the steep city sidewalk, the early morning sunshine warming the nape of his neck, a trickle of sweat dampening the back of his moisture-wicking running shirt.

He'd Googled Eve's home address—not without difficulty—and decided to work it into his morning run. It felt sort of stalker-ish, but at the same time he wanted to make sure she was okay. He didn't know her well, but even he knew something bigger was wrong. She'd been on edge since she'd picked him up at the hotel last night. He'd thought it was about the design, and maybe it was, but it certainly wasn't the whole story.

It's always the woman's fault, never the man's, Eve had said.

It still felt personal. But he no longer thought it was personal toward him.

He'd run by her house and at least make sure her car was in the driveway, he told himself.

As he ran, he tried to take note of the different architectural styles he saw. While it was true that the city had a certain period feel to it, as he moved away from the downtown business district, he saw more and more examples of multicultural influences. For centuries, people from all over the world had immigrated to Canada through this port city, and those who'd settled here had left their marks. He had no doubt he could design the perfect City Hall to reflect the city's diverse history, yet still give his uncle a modern, trademark Matt Brison building.

Eve's tidy little two-story house was located in an aging neighborhood of starter homes for young, upwardly mobile professional couples. Station wagons and minivans speckled the driveways of its steep, winding streets. Latticework fences, intertwined with creeping vines and scrubby underbrush, divided property lots. Ash, maple, poplar, and juniper sprouted in rocky, grass-retardant backyards.

And Eve, dressed in a pair of coveralls, with what appeared to be wood shavings in her ponytailed hair, was standing in a flowerbed at the side of her house, staring up at a window. It seemed she was an early riser, too.

He mopped at his forehead with the crease of his elbow, glad that the morning was cool and he wasn't sweating too much. The breeze off the harbor kept the temperature down.

"Lose another earring?" he called to her from the safety of the sidewalk. He didn't want to take her by surprise—not until he'd found out what kind of self-defense lessons her brother had given her and how warm she was feeling toward him that morning.

Eve spun around, and Matt blinked. Her coveralls were layered in a thick coating of sawdust and drywall spatters, and the dark circles under her eyes were big enough to cut the glare of a supernova.

He was doubly glad he hadn't crept up on her. At this point, he doubted her nerves could survive it.

Eve didn't answer his question. Instead, she scrambled over the clematis and cut him off at the corner of the house, as if there were something she was trying to keep him from seeing. Before he had time to wonder about that though, she'd tilted her chin upward and pinned him with those deep, dark-lashed eyes.

"I am *really* sorry about last night," she said, looking so angelic that Matt might have been fooled if he didn't have reason to know better. He was learning more about her all the time, and while she might be cute, she was definitely no angel. "I have no idea why I behaved the way I did."

He thought that she did but didn't want to explain it. And he thought it best not to pry.

"I came to apologize to you, too," he said. "Oh, yeah," he added, patting at the side pocket of his running shorts, "and to return your twenty dollars."

"You don't have to do either. I deserve to pay your cab fare after ditching you like that in the dark and the rain."

The blaze of Eve's smile left Matt bordering on tongue-tied. She really was cute.

He tried to shake it off with a joke. "In that case, you owe me money. Twenty dollars didn't quite cover it."

"I'll have to write you a check." Eve bounced her house keys in the palm of her hand, indecision etched all over her face. There was a palpable moment of awkward silence. "Or would you settle for a cup of coffee instead?"

Matt resisted the urge to reach over and pick the wood shavings from her hair, only because he didn't want her to withdraw that offer of coffee. Her hesitation suggested she wasn't enthusiastic about it, but he was suddenly very curious about how the inside of her home would look.

"Coffee sounds good," he said, and followed her across the lawn, up her front steps, and into a small entryway.

She closed the door behind them, bent over and unlaced her steel-toed work boots, then dropped them in a corner.

"I'll just put the coffee pot on," she said. "Why don't you have a seat in the living room?"

The living room was off the foyer to the left, a comfortable room filled with overstuffed antique furniture. Photos of family littered the tables and walls. It was a woman's room, and not at all what Matt had expected. He thought of his own sparse condo, with its geometric furniture and early Ellsworth Kelly original artwork. Eve's tastes couldn't be more different than his if she'd made a deliberate effort to make them so. Yet, despite Eve's busy work schedule, her house managed to look like a home, while Matt's condo looked like…

Like it had been designed by an architect. One who spent most of his time at the office.

An open scrapbook displayed on the coffee table caught his eye, and he picked it up. He could hear Eve rattling around in the kitchen. She returned a few moments later, pausing between the yawning double glass doors.

"The coffee will be ready in a minute. I'm just going to run up and change my clothes."

Matt's eyes followed her up the stairwell. Even in coveralls and a layer of sawdust, there was no mistaking that Eve was a beautiful woman. He shook his head. Despite her little idiosyncrasies, he was definitely attracted to her.

Physically, it made sense. It was healthy and normal. What he couldn't quite figure out was what she intended to do with the baseball bat she was clutching in a white-knuckled hand.

Chapter Five

Eve was glad Matt had happened along while she was still trying to work up the nerve to enter the house. Having him downstairs made it easier to keep calm when the mess in her bedroom left her anything but that.

Tossing the bat onto the bed, she clamped her eyelids shut, then popped them open, but nothing had changed. Her panties still dangled from the lampshade.

The remainder of her clothing littered the bedroom floor, and a large, cedar-lined oak wardrobe sprawled drunkenly facedown on top of her great-grandmother's antique hooked rug. A copy of Eve's final divorce decree was skewered to her pillow with a finish nail.

She spun in a slow, incredulous circle and stared at the chaos around her, then curled her fingers into fists. She plucked the nail from the pillow and inspected the antique linen pillowcase. There was a small hole. Blinking back angry tears, she crumpled the divorce decree and crammed it into the back pocket of her coveralls. She stooped to grasp the front end of the wardrobe. One sharp corner screeched against the hardwood floor as she tried to lift it.

Matt's voice drifted up from the foot of the stairs. "Is

everything all right?"

Releasing her hold on the wardrobe, Eve bit her lip. She could ask him for help. She probably should. But they had to work together, and she wasn't sure she could trust him to keep this to himself.

"Everything's fine," she called back, listening until she heard him move back into the living room.

Then she did a quick search of the rest of the upstairs, although she already knew Claude was gone. He wouldn't want to be caught in the act. He wanted to send her a message, and he knew she'd never been good at his games.

The upstairs was empty, just as she'd expected. She went back to her room, dragged a brush through her snarled hair and, showering wood chips onto the floor, re-fashioned her long, curly ponytail, then changed into shorts and a T-shirt she'd grabbed off the floor. Clicking the bedroom door firmly shut behind her, she pattered down the stairs in her bare feet.

Matt lounged on the flowered sofa right where she'd left him, his massive male presence looking ridiculously comfortable amidst the damask cabbage roses. He was flipping through the pages of a scrapbook that contained clippings of past projects Eve had consulted on—none of which were likely to impress a brilliant architect of his caliber.

Uneasy prickles chased up her spine. Eve quickly was reminded that she knew enough brilliant men to last her a lifetime. Matt seemed harmless enough, but so did they all, at least at first.

"How would you like your coffee?" she asked.

He didn't lift his head from his reading. "Black, please."

She carried two steaming mugs back to the living room and placed them on the low pine coffee table, nudging aside a glass trifle dish piled high with more of the family photos her mother kept sending her. Eve then chose an easy chair to sit in—the one farthest away from the sofa.

Matt snapped the scrapbook shut and held it up. His thick-lashed blue eyes met hers, warm and sincere. "Your work is good."

Eve would have to be flatlining not to appreciate a compliment of her work, especially from Matt Brison. It was the warmth of his gaze, however, that made her want to burst into tears.

Her home had just been trashed, and she'd like nothing better than to throw herself into a friendly pair of arms and let someone else deal with the mess. But Eve was stronger than that.

"Thank you," she said, amazed by how calm she sounded.

"There's no reason why we can't work together on the City Hall project," Matt continued, tapping the scrapbook thoughtfully. "Maybe even brainstorm a little. I told you, I'm always open to suggestions."

She lifted her coffee cup to her unsteady lips and concentrated on business. She couldn't resist poking him a little, just to see if he'd laugh. She could use one herself.

"You don't have any ideas of your own?" she said.

He slumped deeper into the sofa and clasped his fingers behind his head, his gaze stroking her from head to toe. A lick of heat leaped into his eyes. "I've got plenty of ideas."

She focused on her coffee and tried not to take his words out of context. Matt was a rich, handsome man, famous in his field, and flirting came naturally to him. It had nothing to do with her.

And no way was she finessing the budget, if that was his game.

"Why don't you just come right out and tell Bob that this project isn't your style and be done with it?" she suggested. "Then you wouldn't have to worry about new ideas."

"I don't know," Matt said slowly, smoothing his chin with the pad of his thumb. He had a nice chin, strong and solid—it went well with the rest of him. The navy running gear showed off a far different frame than the one she'd expected based on his business suits. "It's been a long time since I've had ideas like this," he added. "They might be well worth exploring."

Eve took a long, flustered swig of coffee and choked on it, burning the inside of her nose. Matt jumped to his feet and thumped her on the back until she feared for a few of her ribs. Then he switched to a gentler rub between her shoulders. Bending forward, he brought his face within inches of hers and dropped his free hand to her bare knee.

"Better?" he asked.

Not really. Now she couldn't breathe at all.

The phone rang.

"Let me grab that for you," Matt said, reaching for the cordless handset since he was closest to it.

Eve couldn't read the caller I.D. from where she was. Panic-stricken, she thought of who might be calling her and settled on the worst-case scenario.

"Let it ring. It's probably my mother." Unless, of course, it was Claude, calling to see if she'd gotten the message he'd left her. That would be the post-apocalyptic scenario.

Matt had already grabbed the phone, though. His apologetic smile as he passed her the receiver seemed to say, *"Isn't that cute? She doesn't want to talk to her mother when there's a man in the house."*

Which was true enough. Eve didn't want her mother getting any of her hopes up. Eve was through with men.

She hit the green Talk button. She'd feel stupid not answering it now.

Her mother's voice came through loud and clear. "Hello, sweetheart. I was wondering…if it rains, we can't have the party outdoors. Do you think we should rent one of those big tents, just in case?"

What Eve thought was that the whole family should have chipped in and sent her parents on a cruise for their fortieth anniversary. But what she said was, "Renting a tent sounds like a good idea."

"And you're sure you're still coming?" her mother finished anxiously, reigniting Eve's all-too-familiar pangs of guilt. She'd blown off too many family functions in the past, and this one was important. Her mother kept calling it a party, when in fact it was more of a family reunion.

"Of course, I'll be there."

"Good. Because there's someone we'd like you to meet."

Eve's guilt gave way to an equally familiar irritation. Her mother couldn't seem to understand that she wasn't interested in meeting men. Her glance drifted to Matt, and she shifted around in her chair to face away from him.

After she said good-bye, she turned to find his clear blue eyes fixed on her. She lowered her own in confusion. It would be too much to hope that he hadn't overheard that last bit of the conversation. Her mother's voice carried, after all.

"My mother thinks marriage is the greatest accomplishment a woman can achieve," Eve said, heat clawing her cheeks. "She's always trying to fix me up with men."

"If it helps matters any, my mother has a thing about marriage, too." Matt laughed without a whole lot of humor. "She's tried it five times. I think she holds the record for the shortest marriages in history." He picked at a loose thread on the arm of the sofa. "People who can't commit shouldn't keep trying."

While Eve found five excessive—one had been more than enough for her—she still felt the need to defend his mother. "Maybe she wants to commit but is having difficulty finding the right man."

Matt's expression conveyed his opinion of that theory. "Don't get me wrong. I love her. But she's done enough comparison shopping to at least be able to find one she can tolerate. I think a person should know what they want and go after it. None of this 'Oops, I made a mistake.' Do a little research beforehand. Whatever happened to 'marriage is forever?' Why else would anyone bother?"

Inside, Eve winced. He had some strong opinions on the matter, but she'd heard too many similar comments from her own family to let that statement pass. *Nobody ever said marriage was supposed to be easy. Couldn't you give it more time? Couldn't you at least try and work things out?*

"Maybe she's looking for that special someone she can respect and admire, and who respects and admires her in return," Eve said.

Matt's dark head tilted slightly sideways, and he stared at her for a long moment. "Is that what you look for in a relationship? Mutual respect and admiration?"

When she'd married Claude, she supposed she'd done so because he'd made her feel respected and admired. At first. And she'd certainly been impressed by him. At first.

She drained the last drops of her coffee and stifled a huge yawn. "I'm not looking for a relationship. I'm quite happy with my life the way it is."

"Huh," Matt said thoughtfully, giving her the distinct impression she'd just disappointed him somehow.

If so, she refused to feel sorry about it. Rebellion kicked in. She was tired of being viewed as a disappointment to others. Didn't anyone ever care that, just maybe, she might be disappointed in them?

. . .

Matt couldn't come up with the right word to describe the swarm of emotions Eve elicited from him.

Confusion, possibly. Irritation, undoubtedly. But it was the view of those short-shorts, tanned legs, and glittery, pink-tipped toenails that had him once more wanting to kiss her.

The silence grew so loud he could hear the ticking of his wristwatch. Until today, he hadn't even known it made any noise.

"Why don't you let me see some of those ideas of yours?" he suggested, changing the topic.

Her eyes widened. "You mean, right now?"

Matt shrugged. "Why not?"

She disappeared with a swish of her ponytail and a flurry of those tempting bare limbs and reappeared moments later, tottering under a stack of papers that required the weight of her chin to keep them from toppling over.

"Here's the first of them." She dumped the papers in his lap. Then, palming a letter opener off a small escritoire, she settled back in her chair and began sorting through a mound of mail, methodically slicing open each envelope. Matt placed a protective hand over his throat.

She paused, the letter opener poised in mid-air, sunlight glinting off its pewter blade. "Something wrong?"

Matt forced his hand away from his throat and picked up the top file. "No, of course not."

"I'll try not to disturb you," she said.

Too late. She'd already disturbed him. Just not in the way she might think.

In spite of that, it wasn't long before he became totally absorbed in the papers in front of him. She was good, he conceded, adding the file he'd just finished to the growing stack on the floor at his feet. Given the proper education and training, she could be great. He stretched the kinks out of limbs stiffened from too much time spent in one position.

Why didn't she do more with her talent?

He started to ask her, then realized she was sound asleep, curled up in the overstuffed chair. The sun no longer shone through the front window, and his stomach told him it was getting close to lunchtime, but she looked so adorable curled up with her hands under her cheek and her tanned knees against her chest that Matt was in no hurry to leave.

She gave a soft sigh, a frown crinkling her delicate brow. The position she was in couldn't be comfortable, yet the shadows under her eyes told him how badly she needed the rest. A tiny knot twisted in Matt's stomach. Could he move her without waking her?

The trill of the phone shattered the quiet. Eve, however, didn't twitch a muscle, which answered Matt's question—he could tap dance beside her, and it wasn't likely to wake her.

The phone persisted, and he debated whether or not he should answer it since she hadn't seemed to want him to before. Then he decided to wait until the answering machine picked up. If it sounded like an emergency, he'd wake her. He glanced doubtfully at her sleeping form. Well, he'd try.

When the machine finally kicked in, however, the caller hung up—then the phone began to ring again almost immediately. Matt listened to this cycle twice more before deciding to answer and put an end to it.

"Hello?" he said, speaking softly even though it seemed unlikely that anything short of dynamite could accomplish disturbing Eve's nap.

There was a brief hesitation on the other end of the line. "Who is this?" a low, male voice demanded. The hair on the back of Matt's neck stood up at the frigid tone of the man's simple words.

"Who is *this*?" he countered. His eyes darted to Eve, still asleep in her chair.

The line went dead then, and Matt stared at the receiver in his hand for a few brief seconds before replacing it in its cradle. He thought about Eve's jumpiness, the dark circles under her eyes, and the baseball bat. He remembered the strange noises coming from her bedroom, as if she'd been rearranging furniture, and the way she hadn't wanted him to answer her phone.

He didn't like the conclusion he was coming to.

He ditched the remaining files on the floor and got to his feet. He couldn't leave her here alone without making sure she'd be okay. First, though, he'd move her to the sofa and make her more comfortable. He slipped one arm beneath her knees, the other under her shoulders, and held his breath, waiting for her to open her eyes and demand to know what he was doing. Her head lolled against his forearm, and her mouth fell open. She snorted daintily, and Matt grinned, wishing he dared drop a kiss on the end of that trim little nose.

The knuckles of her limply dangling hand brushed his thigh, and he dumped her on the sofa as if she'd suddenly burst into flames. She sighed, rolled over, and mumbled something under her breath. Matt's heart pounded hard in his chest. It was probably, "*Get a life.*"

The sooner he checked her house and got out, the better.

He started in the kitchen.

The patio doors leading to a small deck were latched. The screen from the open window above the kitchen table, however, rested against one wainscoted wall, and a tiny clod of dirt clung to the sill. Matt remembered Eve standing under that same window when he'd arrived, then the way she'd rushed to meet him—as if there were something she didn't want him to see…

A quick glance outside confirmed his suspicions. There

were two man-sized footprints planted squarely in the flowerbed.

Someone had broken into her house.

Matt followed a trail of dried dirt to the second floor. The first room at the head of the stairs was the bathroom, where everything seemed to be in its proper place. It smelled nice, he noted. Very feminine.

He then eased open the door across the hall and peered inside. His chin went slack. She'd sat drinking coffee with him, discussing business as calm as could be, when she'd known all along what was waiting for her upstairs. Had it even occurred to her to ask him for help? Maybe trust him a little?

At least now he knew why it had sounded like she was moving furniture. She must have tried to lift that wardrobe by herself. It was a huge, heavy piece, another antique, and one she'd never be able to move.

He needed to be doing something physical. After a few moments of grunting and swearing, he had the wardrobe upright. He checked it over for damage, rubbing a hand down one side, feeling the thick grain of the wood. Not a scratch on it.

Pausing to catch his breath, he spied the black dress she'd worn the night before lying on the floor near her discarded coveralls. Flecks of sawdust clung to its filmy fabric.

He pressed his thumbs against his eyelids. She must have had that dress on underneath her coveralls, which explained why she was so tired. He'd bet big money she'd spent the night at a construction site.

Had she called the police?

Probably not. From what he'd seen of her, she was just stubborn enough to try and deal with this herself.

Preoccupied, he hung her coveralls on a hook on the back of the bedroom door. As he did so, a crumpled wad of paper bounced off the toe of his shoe. He picked it up, smoothing it between his palms while he tried to think of what he should do. He couldn't leave her alone without first finding out what was going on, but he wasn't likely to find out from Eve.

He went to re-crumple the paper when bold lettering at the top of it caught his eye. He inspected the paper more closely. Then, carefully, he wadded it up again and tucked it back in the pocket of her coveralls.

He'd been right. It was personal. And now he knew why she was so touchy about failed relationships.

. . .

The lazy drone of a fly and its feather-light touch on her bare arm penetrated Eve's state of semi-consciousness.

She pried open one eye. Streetlight streamed through the soft drapery of the long, narrow, eastward-facing living room windows. She shot upright and struggled to get her bearings, rubbing her eyes and blinking a few times. It couldn't be night, could it?

The house was silent except for the fly, and she sent up a swift prayer of thanks. Her teeth had fur, she hadn't had a shower yet today, and her head ached. She threw back a blanket and realized Matt must have covered her with it before he left. Mortification consumed her. She couldn't believe she'd fallen asleep on him.

Then, she smelled the coffee. She must have forgotten to turn off the coffee maker that morning. She swung her feet to the floor and made a mad dash to the kitchen, hoping it hadn't scorched to the bottom of the pot.

She rounded a corner and smacked into something solid standing in front of the refrigerator. Large hands grabbed her by the elbows, lifting her, and she let out a frightened squeak.

"I know I haven't had a shave yet, but I didn't think I looked all that bad," Matt said, setting her back on her feet.

Eve's heart rate slowed to a steady jackhammer pace as she tried to gather her scattered wits. She finally noticed that the kitchen lights were on, and in their white glare, he didn't look bad at all. In fact, he looked great. His long, lean body, stubbled chin, and intense blue eyes dominated her whole kitchen.

He still wore his running gear.

"Have you been here all day?" she asked, incredulous, her sleep-fogged brain not operating at one hundred percent. God, she hoped her breath didn't smell as bad as it tasted.

"I figured I might as well stay. You were asleep, and it was nice and quiet here." His unwavering eyes fastened on hers. "And I had a lot of reading to do."

Eve remembered all the files she'd dumped on him. At least he'd put his time to good use.

A box on the kitchen table caught her attention. Her voice rose an octave. "You ordered *pizza*?"

"It was either that or eat peanut butter on pita bread, which was all I could find in your cupboards. I saved you some," he added.

"I haven't had time to buy groceries lately." Eve tried to figure out how she'd slept through a pizza delivery. She didn't know whether to be embarrassed or annoyed. "You're probably in a hurry to get back to your hotel," she said.

If so, no one would ever know it. He propped one hip against the tiled countertop. "Could I have a cup of coffee first?"

He'd made fresh coffee.

Eve was at a complete loss as to how to handle this situation. It wasn't often she had architects sit around her house and watch her sleep. The clock over the kitchen sink chimed the hour. It was ten o'clock. At night.

She began to back out of the kitchen, bumping into a wall in the process. "Of course. Have your coffee. But I need to grab a shower. I'm sure you could use one, too." The twist of his lips made her wish she'd thought her words through. "Would you mind letting yourself out when you're finished?"

"With the coffee or the shower?" he asked.

Eve didn't dignify that with a response. She turned and raced for the stairs, taking them two at a time, then skidded to a stop at her open bedroom door.

Her wardrobe was back in its proper place and her clothes were all neatly folded and stacked in piles on her bed.

Including her underwear.

She felt her whole body blush, right from the soles of her feet to the roots of her hair. He'd put his time to even better use than she'd thought.

Her black dress was draped across the foot of her bed, and her breath caught. The dress had been with her coveralls, and in her coveralls was her divorce decree. She scrambled around until she found the coveralls, then searched the pockets for the document. She found it, then took it and tossed it in the trash. She had her own copy in a security box at her bank.

Maybe Matt hadn't seen it.

Her lips trembled. The last thing she wanted was to answer questions about Claude, especially from a man who was critical of his own mother's poor judgment in men.

She grabbed clean clothes, fled to the bathroom, locked the door, stripped, and hurled herself into the shower. Hot water streamed over her as she rested her aching forehead against the glass enclosure. Her brief marriage was a mistake she thought she'd put behind her, but circumstances were suddenly making it impossible for her to keep it there.

When she was scrubbed and freshly dressed in skinny

jeans and a clean T-shirt, she pattered slowly downstairs to see if Matt had taken her not-so-subtle hint and gone back to his hotel.

He hadn't. He was reading the newspaper at her kitchen table, his large fingers scrunching its edges into fan-like wrinkles. She steeled herself for a lot of questions she didn't want to answer as he pushed the pizza box across the table toward her.

"Hungry?" he asked.

"Starved."

She eyed the box greedily, trying to remember when she'd last eaten, then took a slice of pizza and bit off a mouthful before pouring herself a cup of coffee with hands that still shook a little. Matt knew her bedroom had been trashed, that she wore multi-colored Brazilian boy-brief underwear, and there was the possibility he knew about Claude, too. She and the architect were certainly becoming well acquainted.

Matt folded the newspaper and set it aside carefully. "Did you know that my hotel room costs three hundred dollars a night?"

The ice maker on the refrigerator gurgled, and Eve frowned, confused, her train of thought interrupted. Whatever she'd expected him to say, that wasn't it.

"If you're worried about money, a room with your uncle would be free," she pointed out cautiously, scarcely able to believe her good luck. If he wasn't going to mention the mess he'd cleaned up in her bedroom, then neither was she.

"I'm not worried about the money because I'm not paying for it. You are." Matt drummed his fingers on the tabletop. "It's coming out of the budget for City Hall."

"Bob is spending three hundred municipal dollars a night on a hotel room rather than put you up himself?" Eve was so outraged she forgot about everything else. "I don't care if he is your uncle. The man's a moron."

"I'm still not convinced *moron* is the right word," Matt mused. "Besides, a hotel room is always in my contract. I like my privacy. I need the space to work in and to be able to keep in touch with my own offices."

She played with the crust of the partially eaten slice of pizza in front of her. "Bob's house is huge. You could have all the privacy you wanted."

Matt raised an eyebrow. "Would you want to stay with him if you had any alternative?"

"Good point," she conceded, and reached for her cup.

"If you want to save budget money, maybe you'd consider renting me a room instead," he suggested.

And Eve, already on edge, upset her coffee all over the newspaper.

Chapter Six

Matt grabbed a handful of paper towels off the roller beside the sink and mopped up the puddle of coffee.

Eve's baffled brain tried to process his suggestion. Rent a room to Matt Brison? Bob Anderson's nephew?

She could think of a dozen reasons why she wasn't going to do it. She'd grown up with three older brothers and a father, and she'd spent two immeasurably long weeks living with an unstable husband. She worked with men every day. Under no circumstances did she want them infiltrating her private space. Her home was where she got away from it all.

But then she remembered her home was no longer a haven, and that ticked her off, which was good. She'd rather be angry than scared.

"Renting me a room makes a lot of sense," Matt was saying. He began to list off his own reasons. "You have a home office already set up. You use the same computer-aided drafting program I do. We'll be working closely together anyway. And," he added after a brief, meaningful pause, "it might not hurt for you to have a roommate around here for a while."

If that was an opening for her to talk about the neatly

folded underwear in her bedroom, Eve wasn't taking it.

"My house isn't very big," she said.

"I won't take up much room. I'll stay out of your way," Matt promised. "Besides, I'll be traveling back and forth to Toronto. You'll never even know I'm around."

Eve felt the first flutters of panic. "I don't cook."

"Believe me, I've already noticed." He lifted the pizza box and wiped up the coffee that had seeped under it. "I don't mind doing the cooking. I'm quite good at it when I have something to work with."

He tossed the soggy paper towels into the proper recycling bin under the counter, earning himself a few roommate points for environmental responsibility.

She already knew what her mother would think if she let him move in, and that shifted the score into a negative range. She shuddered inside. And after Bob had found them trampling his bushes, she had a good idea what he'd think, too.

And then there was Claude.

That scored Matt the winning goal. Maybe he was right. Maybe it would be a good idea for her to have a roommate for a while.

Eve tried to ignore the knot of nervous tension building at the nape of her neck. His reasons for moving in made more sense than hers for keeping him out. It would be a temporary situation. She'd save budget money. She'd have someone around in case Claude came back. She might even get a decent meal or two out of it, without having to use speed dial.

And she might be able to convince Matt not to design some awful steel monstrosity that would get Sullivan Construction in trouble with the zealous public action groups determined to preserve the historic integrity of the city.

Relief evaporated her tension. Those were all good reasons for letting him stay. They'd be roommates. It was no big deal.

She had a mental flash of how he might look coming out of her shower, dressed in nothing but a towel.

"Okay," she said. "But we need to set some house rules."

· · ·

House rules, Eve discovered, could only cover so much.

Even after a few days of trying to get used to Matt, she still wasn't comfortable sharing her space. She used any excuse she could find to spend even less time at home than she had before he moved in.

The other volunteers at the youth center's Internet café had trickled out around suppertime, but Eve had wanted to finish this one last coat of paint so she could start cutting trim for the large, street-front windows.

Fumes from the thinner stung her nose as she stirred a can of ecru paint beneath the bright glare of a bare, 100-watt bulb in the soon-to-be main meeting area. She poured the paint into a tray and dipped her roller, ignoring the prickling sensations between her shoulder blades. She'd done this dozens of times in the past, but it was getting late, and it wasn't the greatest neighborhood for catching a cab. She'd gotten a ride here with one of the other volunteers and hadn't planned on staying after everyone else left, but she didn't want to go home too early, either.

She ran the roller as far up the wall as she could reach, tiny paint drops splattering her coveralls. She couldn't deny it felt good having someone else in the house with her at night. She wasn't always listening for every little noise, and so far Matt was an exemplary roommate. He was tidy, unobtrusive, and fed himself.

That meant the problem had to be her. She felt awkward

around him, not so much uneasy as a bit too aware of his presence. She wasn't sure why. He'd done nothing wrong.

Maybe that was it. He was a little too perfect, and she was waiting for the illusion to crack.

Shortly before midnight, she finally called it a night and packed in her roller. The building groaned as she tapped the lid back on the can of paint.

She could no longer ignore the creaking sounds the old building made or the sensation of being inside a giant goldfish bowl. Blinds on those large, open windows would be a nice touch. She made a mental note to approach Bob for a personal donation. If he could toss away three hundred municipal dollars a night on a hotel room for his nephew, then he could find some spare change of his own for window treatments for a youth project that he'd initiated.

The building groaned again, and Eve stiffened, along with the fine hairs on the backs of her arms. The large windows reflected the café's interior, but through the reflection a slight movement caught her eye. Someone was lurking in the shadows across the street, watching her.

Chunks of construction debris crunched beneath her boot heels as she dashed to flip off the lights, plunging the room into a thin darkness illuminated only by the faint glow from the streetlights outside. She was going to talk to Bob about the lack of decent lighting in this ratty neighborhood when she approached him about the blinds. No wonder it had such a lousy reputation.

She ducked behind a large stack of unused Gyprock sheets, telling herself not to panic. Maybe she'd imagined the movement, although her instincts screamed that she hadn't.

With construction dust tickling her nose, she felt around until she found the nail gun she'd left on the floor. There was no way she was going to wait for a cab now. The driver would be in no hurry to come to this neighborhood at this time of night.

Eve grew angry then, but mostly at herself. She wasn't big, she wasn't all that strong, but she wasn't defenseless, either. She wasn't going to cower in the darkness and wait for something to happen.

She clutched the nail gun to her chest and glanced at the luminous dial on her watch. Then she found her briefcase and Blackberry, hesitated for a moment, and reluctantly punched in some numbers.

...

Matt propped his feet on the coffee table and prepared to take a bite of his salami sandwich, checking his watch for what must have been the fiftieth time and wondering where Eve might be so late at night.

Sharing a house with her wasn't turning out quite the way he'd anticipated. He'd given her three days to get used to him, and still, Eve didn't observe any of the common courtesies normally extended when two people cohabited. She didn't tell him where she was going. She didn't call when she was going to be late. And he found her habit of drying her delicates on the curtain rod in the shower to be more than a little disconcerting. He couldn't get fantasies involving lacy panties out of his head.

What bothered him the most, however, was that she'd never mentioned the break-in, the trashed bedroom, or the crumpled-up divorce decree.

And the wary way she watched him made him very careful of the way he treated her. Whatever had gone wrong in her marriage, Eve had been burned, and despite Matt's best efforts, she didn't want to trust him.

He balanced the sandwich and plate on his stomach and chewed thoughtfully.

She didn't have to trust him, but it was about time he insisted she show him a little consideration. They didn't need to advertise he was living with her, but he should have worked it into the house rules that he had no intention of being treated like a dirty secret.

His uncle's reaction to him moving out of the hotel hadn't been much more encouraging than Eve's. When Matt had explained to him it was a matter of convenience, that Eve had all the equipment he needed in her home office, Uncle Bob had been indifferent.

"You don't have to explain anything to me, Mattie," he'd said. "Never in a million years would I think there'd be any other reason for you to be rooming with Eve."

Matt had no idea what that comment was supposed to mean.

He'd given up trying to work. He had the design well in hand, although he wasn't about to let frugal little Eve get a look at it yet. He didn't want her complaining about the budget before his uncle had the funding in place. Besides, Matt had some ideas of his own as to where to cut costs. She was in for a surprise. And he was prepared to be entertained by that, because it was no big secret that Eve liked to win.

He polished off the sandwich and headed into the kitchen to get a glass of water. The phone rang as he walked by, and he grabbed it, breaking the third house rule on Eve's one-sided list. The small act of rebellion gave him a sense of satisfaction. "Hello?"

"I'm sorry. I must have the wrong number," a woman said.

Matt wondered if he should identify himself, then decided against it. Let Eve do her own explaining.

"If you're looking for Eve, then this is the right number.

But she's not home right now."

"Oh." A long silence. Then, "This is her mother. Could you tell Eve her father and I are coming up to the city for a few days at the end of the month? We thought we'd stay with her, but if there isn't a spare room…"

In a two-bedroom house there wasn't likely to be, but he could always move back into a hotel for a few days. He could even fly back to Toronto to do some business in his office, something he'd been putting off because he hadn't wanted Eve to be alone in the house. This might provide the perfect opportunity.

"There's plenty of room," he said. "She'd love to have you stay here." He figured the odds on that being true were fifty-fifty. Okay, maybe not that high.

"We'll look forward to meeting you, then," her mother said.

That sounded ominous. Maybe Eve's rule about not answering the phone was a good one after all.

He shrugged it off, but the next time the phone rang, he waited for the answering machine to pick it up.

"Matt? Are you there?" Eve's voice was muffled, like she was in a closet or maybe whispering.

Matt's heart bounced like a basketball off his rib cage. Something was wrong or she wouldn't be calling for him. He snatched up the receiver.

"Where are you?" he asked. "You sound funny."

"At a job site, working on some renovations. I was going to walk home, but hadn't planned to be here so late. My car keys are on a hook by the front door. I don't suppose you could come and get me?"

That threw him. Had she been working late at construction sites for the entire past week?

He scraped his fingers through his hair. "Are you okay?"

"I'm fine. I can always call a cab, but I'd rather not if you can come instead. Cabbies don't really like to come down here at this time of night, and sometimes you have to wait a long time to find one who will."

As she reeled off the address for him, Matt wrestled with an overwhelming urge to shout at her. He might not know the city well, but he read the papers, and he knew the parts to steer clear of. The fact it was hard to get a cab there at night should have told her a few things. One of them was that she shouldn't be walking around that area in daylight, either.

He could yell at her later. The important thing now was to get her home. And when he did, her house rules were going to undergo some serious modifications.

He didn't know how long it would take him to get to her, but he made a quick estimate, wanting to give her some sort of reassurance and a timeframe. She sounded afraid—and that terrified him.

"I'll be there in twenty minutes."

...

He made it in less than ten.

He parked the car in front of a fire hydrant, ran to the building entrance, grabbed the heavy steel door, and jerked it open. Why wasn't the door locked? And what had happened to all the lights?

A fiery pain blossomed in his leg and exploded upward into his groin, doubling him over. He heard a sharp cry and the sound of something heavy as it hit the floor, then Eve was at his side, both of her small hands scrabbling at his shirtsleeve.

"Are you okay?" she asked, anxious.

Matt clamped a hand over whatever was now embedded in the inner flesh of his right thigh. He felt cold sweat beading on his forehead and trickling down his back.

"No. I'm not. Put a light on, will you?"

As bright light flooded the room, he took quick inventory. There was surprisingly little blood, and although his leg hurt like hell, the nail didn't seem to have hit anything vital. Just an inch or two higher, however, and he'd be singing a different tune—and in a higher key.

He spotted the nail gun on the floor, then looked at her in disbelief. "You *shot* me."

"You said you'd be here in twenty minutes," she wailed, wringing her hands. "How was I supposed to know it was you storming through that door?"

"Process of elimination?" Matt tore the fabric of his pants to free the nail head and get a better look at the puncture wound. "You must have some idea of how long it takes to get here from your house. What did you think I was doing—taking the scenic route?"

"Maybe you were going to stop for a hamburger or something. Maybe you were going to take a shower first. Maybe you were in the middle of something important. I didn't know!" Her eyes grew wide and fat teardrops trembled on her lashes. "You said *twenty minutes!*"

"Eve." He leaned against the wall, counted to ten, and tried to remember what he was doing there in the first place. "When a woman calls me from a high-crime neighborhood in the middle of the night, *nothing* is more important. I don't take the time to stop for a hamburger or a shower or anything else." Then he asked the question he believed to be the most important, given the circumstances. "What were you doing hiding in the dark with a nail gun?"

"Old buildings make strange noises. It sounded like someone was walking around in here. I got nervous." Eve's soft brown eyes swam in her pale, elfin face. "And I thought I saw someone watching me through the front window. I turned off the lights so he couldn't see in."

"Why didn't you lock the door instead, so he couldn't *get* in?"

"I didn't want to be locked in with anyone, either…in case someone was already inside."

That made sense.

Whoever had been watching Eve, if he was still out there, he could certainly see everything now. Matt discovered he didn't like the idea of being spied on any better than Eve had.

He gave up. He wasn't going to yell at her for working alone. Not at the moment, when he had something more important to do first.

Her whole body shook as she reached for her briefcase. "I'll drive you to the hospital."

"In a minute." Injured or not, if there was someone inside the building, Matt planned on kicking butt.

Ignoring the pain in his leg, he limped through every room in the main floor of the building. Eve clung close to him, her fingers twisted in the tail of his untucked shirt, hammering home to him without words just how spooked she'd really been. The thought of her crouched in the dark—afraid and armed only with a nail gun for protection—filled him with helpless fury. And if he felt that way, how helpless must Eve be feeling?

There was a kitchen with a storage room and a locked rear entrance, the main meeting area with the enormous street-front window, and two single-unit washrooms. There was no access to the upper levels of the building from inside. The place was empty.

"Can we go now?" she asked when they arrived back in the main room.

"Just one more minute."

Matt took her by the hand and hobbled over to the large

front window, then turned to stare down into her upturned face.

Her tear-dampened eyes glistened with such a look of remorse, he wanted nothing more than to wipe it away. She shouldn't be sorry. If the person spying on her tonight was the same one who'd broken into her house, it was time he learned that Eve didn't have to defend herself. Not anymore. And if that person was her ex-husband, it might help for him to think Eve was now off-limits.

Matt cupped her cheeks between his palms, threading his fingers through her hair. The rich, silky strands were smooth and cool against his skin. This time, he hoped her trembling had nothing to do with fear.

"Matt, this isn't such a good idea," she began, correctly interpreting his intention. She tried to pull back. "Anyone outside can see us."

"That's the whole point."

Matt had been waiting for this moment ever since the night he'd missed his chance in the bushes at his uncle's fundraiser. Now he had a perfectly legitimate excuse. He covered her mouth with his own and cut off her words, intending only to put on a show for whoever might be lurking outside.

He was unprepared for the knife of desire that stabbed through him, hot and hard. He was unprepared for a lot of things, like her warmth and the delicate touch of her fingers as they stole around his waist to smooth the sensitive spot at the base of his spine. Or the heady way sawdust smelled when mixed with the tantalizing scent of a woman. His tongue flitted briefly over her lips before plunging deeper, his fingers twisting in her hair.

But what threw him the most was the sudden, soul-deep conviction that Eve, prickly and unpredictable, and without a domestic bone in her body, was the woman he wanted.

The subtle shift of her hip jarred the nail lodged in his thigh, and a small groan escaped him. She broke away and backed up a step, the rapid rise and fall of her breasts beneath her ridiculous flannel shirt telling him she wasn't unaffected, although her eyes were cautious now.

"What was that for?" she asked, suspicion sharpening her tone.

Matt cleared a throat that felt like it had been rubbed raw with sandpaper. He might want Eve, but she didn't want him. Not yet.

"So that whoever's watching will think you've got a man in your life," he said. "Since we're already living together, I guess that makes me the likeliest candidate."

"We aren't 'living together,'" she pointed out, her eyes darkening. "We're roommates."

A lone car hummed by on the street outside, the reflection of its headlights bouncing off the far wall. It seemed she found simply the idea of living with him distasteful. Good thing Matt's ego was healthy.

"Call me what you want," he said, "but you may as well take advantage of me as long as I'm around."

She muttered something that sounded sort of like, "Men" and "marking their territory."

"What was that?" he asked, but she shook her head.

"All I wanted was a ride home." She reached once again for her briefcase. "Now," she said briskly. "Do you want me to take you to Emergency, or were you planning to remove that nail by yourself? Because I have a pair of vice-grips around here somewhere if you'd like to borrow them."

If their situations were reversed, she would undoubtedly remove the nail from her own leg. With her teeth. Matt weighed trying to impress her against the amount of extra pain it would involve.

"Emergency," he said.

...

The crowded Emergency room was hot and smelled of unwashed bodies. The bright fluorescent lights were blinding as Matt registered, then limped to a vacant chair. Eve was forced to sit across from him, and he made a careful assessment of the other patients in the room.

He might be the only patient with a nail in him, but he doubted if he were the only one who'd been shot. It was a toss-up if Eve would be safer here with him or at home with her new security system.

"You don't have to wait with me," he told her, leaving the decision up to her.

"I shot you," she said. "I should at least keep you company." The man on her left got up and moved. She smiled at Matt, patting the now-empty seat. "Care to join me?"

This was going to be a long night.

Several hours later, Matt's name was called. He eased himself off his chair.

"You coming?" he asked Eve.

The nurse who'd called his name looked at the form in her hand, then addressed Eve. "Immediate family only. Are you family?"

Matt wasn't about to leave her in that waiting room by herself. She might not have noticed it, but there was a three-hundred-pound, tattooed, pro-wrestler type eyeing her with open interest. Matt laced his fingers through hers and hauled her to her feet. "She's my wife."

The nurse tapped the line in question with her finger. "You've listed your mother as your next-of-kin."

"Apron strings," Eve said. "He can't seem to cut them."

Her comment earned a few laughs from the people around her, and Matt's face warmed. Did she always have to have an answer for everything?

The nurse shook her head back and forth, jowls bouncing, and slipped her clipboard under one ample arm.

"Honey, all men are the same. A little boo-boo and they want their mommies." She hustled them through a swinging door, then behind a curtain. "I'll just leave you here, and you can help your husband get his pants off."

This wasn't how Matt had envisioned the first time Eve helped him out of his pants. He waited until the nurse left, then said, "You can turn your back."

"Oh, please." Eve rolled her eyes. "I grew up with three brothers. If you have anything I don't already know about, I'll be sure and tell you."

He was sure she would—and probably everyone else within earshot. He was also certain that his own reaction to having her see him without his pants on would be entirely different than any reaction from her brothers. He didn't need that commented on, either.

"Turn your back," he growled.

With a little sniff and a lift of her slender shoulders, she did as she was told. Matt eased the torn pants off, got on the stretcher, and pulled a thin sheet over his hips and legs. It was bad that he had to be half-naked in front of Eve right then— he wasn't even wearing a hospital gown.

A young resident came in, took one look under the sheet, then sent Eve to the other side of the curtain.

"You're going to need a tetanus shot when we're finished," he said to Matt. The nurse returned with a tray of instruments, and the doctor selected one. He held it aloft and flexed it.

"Hang on. This is going to hurt you a lot more than it hurts me."

Chapter Seven

How much Demerol had they given him, anyway?

The first bright-red streaks of dawn shot skyward over the horizon as Eve steered Matt from the car to the front steps, wiping the back of her hand across her forehead. He was every bit as heavy as he looked.

"*Please*, Matt. You'll have to lift a leg if you're going to get up these stairs," she panted. She draped his arm around her shoulders, wrapped both of hers around his waist, and braced herself against his substantial body mass. "You're going to have to help me out a little."

If he didn't, she'd have to leave him passed out on the doorstep until the neighbors got up. Sticking a beer can in his hand would make a nice touch.

She didn't dare laugh for fear she'd cry. This was all her fault. She'd never been afraid of working alone on a job site before. She'd done it dozens of times in the past.

Matt swayed, nearly knocking Eve off her feet. "I can do this myself." He seized the wrought-iron railing in both hands and hauled himself up a step. "See?"

She held her breath and prayed he wouldn't fall backward. If he did, she'd never get him off the ground. He outweighed her by at least sixty pounds, maybe more.

They made it through the front door. He studied the flight of stairs in the foyer, frowning in concentration.

"I can climb those if I hurry." He slumped back against the wall. "But you'd better go up first," he added. "If I fall on you, I'll probably kill you."

He had a point. His movements grew more and more sluggish with every step, and Eve held her breath until he reached the top. She made an executive decision. Her room was the closest to the stairs and the bathroom. For the time being, he could sleep in there.

She helped him swing his legs onto her bed, then softened at the sight of him sprawled across the quilted bedspread, his dark head propped on her lace-trimmed, embroidered pillows. *My hero*.

Guilt gnawed at her. He'd come running to her rescue, and what had she done? She'd shot him. If she hadn't panicked, none of this would have happened. If she hadn't been avoiding him, none of this would have happened, either. When had she become such a wimp?

"Let me get these pants off you," she said, reaching for the button at his waist. Her fingers brushed the crisp hairs on his stomach as she eased his zipper down. *Oh my God*. She was getting turned on by undressing a drugged and helpless man. How sad was that?

Matt's heavy eyelids drooped. He reached over and touched her cheek. "Somehow, I'd pictured this moment differently."

And men said women were teases. She should kiss him the way he'd kissed her at the café, then tell him it was all for show, and see how he liked it.

But if he could kiss her that way for show, Eve hated to think what it would be like if he kissed her for real. She grabbed the cuffs of his pant legs and pulled.

"You know," she puffed, "you could help."

A sexy, lazy look spread over his chiseled, unshaven face. "If I could help, this would have a totally different outcome."

She almost tumbled backward off the bed. That was the Demerol talking. She shouldn't pay too much attention to anything he said for the next few hours.

"Don't bet on it," she said, regaining her balance. "You're like any one of my brothers." Eve finished wrestling his pants off, then snapped her swinging jaw shut. He wore navy boxer briefs. She'd thought male models in underwear ads were the only men who looked good in them, but she was wrong. If not for the thick, white bandage around the top of one long, muscular thigh, he'd look like a model himself. To think he'd wasted all that on architecture.

She dragged the covers over him, then flopped on the bed beside him and thumped his chest with her fist. "You're useless, too."

"I've never had any complaints before." Matt trapped her fist on his chest with one warm hand, and her heart shivered. He twisted onto his side so his face rested scant inches from hers. He touched a free finger to the tip of her nose on his third try. "And I am not like your brothers. Although they probably share a lot of my fr…" The word gave him a little difficulty. "Fr…frustration. Did they get mad at you much when you were little?"

"Never." Eve reclaimed her hand and sat up, shoving the image of those boxer briefs out of her mind. "They adored me. Still do. Then again," she amended, "their adoration needs to be put in perspective. These are the same guys who once tried to use me as shark bait."

A dimple worked at the corner of his mouth. "They did not."

"It's true," Eve insisted, wondering if she could get that dimple to flicker into a full-blown smile. In all fairness, she probably owed him at least a smile or two right now. "When I was seven years old my older brother Cyril took me down to the harbor at high tide, tied a rope around me, and he and his friends hung me off the end of the wharf because they wanted to see if they could catch a shark. They told me we were playing Peter Pan and I got to be Tinker Bell because I was the cutest. My two younger brothers stood back and watched."

Matt's face creased into the smile she'd been aiming for. "Did they catch anything?"

"Of course not. Sharks don't come that close to land. Even if they did, they'd be more interested in fish than skinny little girls."

Matt shifted one broad shoulder into a more comfortable position and closed his eyes. Just when she thought he was about to drift off, the corners of his mouth arced upward again.

"What was their reasoning for hanging Tinker Bell by a rope over the water?" he asked, his words threaded and slurred.

"So she'd have a soft landing if the fairy dust wore off."

He laughed out loud. "I missed out on a lot, being an only child. It must have been nice growing up with people who were so concerned for your safety."

"It's easy to tell you don't have any brothers," Eve said. "They were disgusted with me for being so gullible."

Matt peeled open one eye. "You were seven."

"I was a savvy seven. Or so I liked to think." She folded his torn, bloodstained pants and laid them at the foot of the bed.

"What other things are you gullible about, Eve?" he

asked softly, trying to focus his eyes on her. "Working alone late at night in bad neighborhoods?" He cocked an eyebrow and glanced down at himself, then at her. "Helping men take their pants off?"

"I only do that for the men I shoot."

"Sooner or later we're going to talk about that, you know," he said softly. "The men you shoot, I mean. Or the ones you'd like to. When I can think straighter."

Matt was right. He deserved an explanation. Then he'd know how right her brothers were to be disgusted with her. But how did she explain a twisted, two-week train wreck of a marriage to Matt, a man who rolled his eyes at his own mother's inability to commit?

She hopped off the bed. "I have to run over to the head office and get some papers, but I'll be back soon. You should be all right by yourself for a bit — as long as you stay in that bed."

"I'm coming with you." Matt tried to sit up. "You aren't going anywhere alone."

She wasn't having him get in the habit of following her around — not that she believed he could do it at the moment, anyway — but it was nice of him to worry. In fact, he was far nicer than she'd given him credit for initially. He'd seemed genuinely concerned when he'd come to her rescue, and not at all angry over her having shot him. He'd been more annoyed that she'd been working late alone in the café.

He was easy to like, and that made her uneasy. She couldn't imagine why Matt should care.

"I'll be back before you know it," she said.

He sagged back against her embroidered pillows, closed his eyes, then cracked them open again. "Okay. But you have one hour, Tinker Bell. Then I call in the Lost Boys."

Eve hoped his sense of humor stayed with him long after

the medication wore off.

...

Early morning traffic was light, and it wasn't long before she walked into her cramped office at Sullivan Construction.

Calling it an office was a flattering overstatement. She was often at job sites, and the company had a conference room for meetings, so she didn't require anything fancy. She had spare rolls of toilet paper stacked under a chair, and a pre-fab maple door, screwed to two sets of folding metal legs, served as her desk. But at least she had a window.

Elevators whirred in the hallway, then office doors opened and closed as the building slowly came to life. Time was wasting. Eve opened her briefcase and began to gather the things she'd need for a few days of working from home.

She had one foot out the door when the phone on her desk rang. She hesitated, then decided she'd better answer it. The hour Matt had given her was more than up, and although common sense told her he'd be dead to the world by now, she wasn't used to looking after other people and didn't want to take that chance. What if he needed her?

Marion Balcom's cheery voice was a relief. "I was hoping you'd be an early bird!"

Eve wasn't. She yawned and glanced at her watch. At the moment, she was more of a late-night person. Really, really late.

She shifted the briefcase from under her arm, letting it slide to the floor. "Hi, Marion. What can I do for you?"

"I was wondering if you could find out for me what's going to happen to the old City Hall."

That was an odd request, since the fate of the building had nothing to do with Eve. "Wouldn't you be better off calling the mayor's office to get that information?"

"You know what Bob's like. Getting anything out of him is like pulling hens' teeth." Marion gave a light, meaningful laugh, and Eve could sympathize. Bob had two sets of rules — one for himself and one for everyone else.

The information wasn't exactly confidential, however, and Eve didn't see any harm in helping. She knew what it was like to be brushed off by people with more important things to do than answer a few simple questions. Besides, Eve still wanted to impress her. Marion Balcom was high up on the food chain with the Department of Tourism and Culture, and she would be a great asset for Eve's career, maybe even make up for the job she lost to Matt. "I'll see what I can do."

She gathered her things and drove home, then tiptoed into her bedroom to check on her houseguest.

He hadn't needed her. Instead, he was sound asleep on his back with one arm flung out to the side, the other stretched above his head, his long body sagging deep into the thick mattress of her double bed. He'd thrown off the quilt, and the white, cotton sheet twined around his hips and legs like honeysuckle around a porch rail.

He didn't look at all like an internationally renowned architect. He looked like an internationally renowned centerfold.

Looking at him like that, she tried not to think about the way he'd kissed her. It wasn't like he'd meant anything by it. He'd only wanted Claude to think she had a new man in her life.

Eve bit her lower lip.

She reached out a reluctant finger, tracing it along the

sweep of his jaw. Matt twitched, rolled onto his side, and let out a soft grunt. Eve snatched her hand back, grabbed her nightgown and bathrobe, then scurried out, easing the door shut behind her.

After shedding her clothes and crawling wearily into the bed in the spare room where Matt normally slept, she snuggled her cheek into a spicy, aftershave-scented pillowcase and fell into a deep, dreamless sleep.

The next thing she knew, someone was pounding on her front door. A travel alarm clock on the chair beside the bed read 11:07 a.m.

Eve pulled the pillow over her head, intending to wait until whoever it was had the decency to get lost, then remembered Matt was asleep, too, and needed the rest far more than she did.

She said a few rude words as she swung her feet to the floor, hauled on her bathrobe, then stumbled down the stairs.

Not even in her worst nightmare would she have expected to find Bob Anderson on her doorstep, wielding an armful of red roses. She clutched the neck of her bathrobe and blinked up at him, but Bob didn't comment on her appearance, although she knew quite well how she looked—like she'd just crawled out of bed.

"These are yours," he said, thrusting the roses at her, the clear cellophane wrapping crackling. "Is Mattie here?"

She was speechless. Why was Bob Anderson bringing her flowers?

He stepped past her into the foyer, casually inspecting his surroundings, and straightened a framed watercolor hanging on the wall. The small gesture irritated Eve. First Claude, now Bob. Men kept touching her private things without permission.

But Bob had every right to visit his nephew, and Eve was

determined to be nice, because for some strange reason, Matt actually liked the mayor.

Bob was looking at her, waiting for some sort of response. What had he asked her?

Something hit the floor above their heads.

"Eve!" Matt shouted. "Where are my pants?"

A ball of ice tumbled into the pit of her stomach as she scanned her memory. They were at the foot of her bed, right where she'd left them.

No way was she going to yell that out in front of Bob.

"How should I know?" she called back.

"Because you had them last."

This would be a good time for some natural disaster to hit. An earthquake, perhaps.

"Matt," she choked out, her voice cracking. "Your uncle's here."

Scuffling and swearing could be heard, and she assumed the Demerol had worn off and his leg was hurting. Either that, or Matt was as excited about Bob's being here as she was. A few seconds later he hobbled to the top of the stairs, zipping his torn, bloodstained trousers over his Jockeys.

Bob's eyes widened. "What the hell happened to you?"

"I shot him," Eve said, tilting her chin up to peer over the fragrant petals in her arms.

"With a nail gun," Matt added. "She was working late last night at a job site. Alone. I surprised her."

Bob frowned at Eve. "You shouldn't be working alone at night," he said. "What's the matter with you?"

Be nice, Eve reminded herself. Bob had a right to be here. But wait until Matt moved out.

"I was working on the Internet café renovations." The ones Bob seemed to have forgotten he'd volunteered her for, she wanted to remind him. "Nights are the only spare time I have. Most of the time I'm not usually alone, but everyone else had to leave early." They all had families. And lives.

The fine lines around Bob's eyes deepened. "They left you alone? Well, it won't be happening again. I'll make sure someone stays with you if you need to work nights."

Matt carefully descended the stairs, favoring his sore leg. "Don't worry about it. For the next little while, Eve and I can operate as a team. Where she goes, I'll go."

Wait just a minute. She had to share her home with him, work with him all day, and now her free time had to be spent with him, too?

No way. Eve had a bad feeling about this. She and Matt spent too much time together as it was, and she wanted more distance. They were crossing that fine line between colleagues and friends, and that line was important. She already liked what she knew of him; she didn't need to know anything more.

Like the fact that he looked incredibly hot in navy blue boxer briefs.

"Or I could just call if I need you," she suggested.

Matt's blue gaze locked with hers.

"Thanks, but I don't have a death wish," he said.

Although right now, death held a certain appeal.

Matt's leg hurt, his mouth was dry from the medication, and he could have used a few more hours of sleep.

He hadn't liked letting her go off alone to the office earlier, and liked it even less that he hadn't been in a position to stop her. Now that the drugs had worn off, however, circumstances had changed. Let Eve argue all she wanted. He was in no mood to listen.

He looked her over, reassuring himself she was okay. Her

hair was a mess, the bathrobe she wore hadn't come from any Victoria's Secret catalog, and the expression on her face warned of storm fronts ahead. She looked rumpled and sexy.

Nothing was going to happen to her.

"You are not following me around," Eve said. The roses in her arms reflected the fire blossoming on her cheeks.

"Of course not." He sat gingerly on a bottom step, easing his injured leg out before him. "I won't have to follow you. We'll be working together."

"I work on a number of projects, not just City Hall. You can't come to all of them."

"I have a laptop. I'm mobile." His leg throbbed. Maybe not as mobile as usual, but mobile nonetheless.

"She says she doesn't want you following her around all day," Uncle Bob interrupted, his voice mild. "There are anti-stalking laws in this country, you know."

Those laws didn't seem to bother Eve's ex-husband.

"Thank you, Bob," Eve said, her tone so sweet Matt almost laughed. She sniffed the flowers in her arms. "And thank you for the roses, too. They're lovely. What's the occasion?"

"Those aren't from me. I found them on the doorstep." Bob plucked an envelope from his suit pocket. "The card says they're from some guy named Claude."

A look of revulsion crossed Eve's face. If there had been any doubt in Matt's mind how she felt about her ex-husband, there was none now. He made a mental note never to bring her roses, too. Besides, Eve was more of a bird-of-paradise kind of woman, all fire and sunbursts. This Claude guy didn't know anything.

Except for how to terrorize a woman. Matt's blood pressure edged up several notches.

Eve handed the flowers back to Bob. "Here. Why don't you give these to your secretary?"

Uncle Bob scooped up the flowers, opened the door, and set them on the doorstep outside, displaying one of his rare moments of tact. Eve, all soft and wide-eyed and mussy-haired, chewed on her lip and looked like she couldn't decide whether or not to burst into tears. Matt hoped she chose not to. If she did, he was going to have to hold her, and she wouldn't like that. Especially in front of his uncle. She tried to seem tough on the surface, but he couldn't shake the image he had of her crouched alone in the dark with only a nail gun for protection.

"Did you have something you wanted me for?" Matt asked, prodding his uncle's memory in an effort to change the subject. The sooner Uncle Bob left the better.

"What?" Uncle Bob appeared confused for a moment as he turned his attention from Eve back to Matt. "Oh, yes." He ran a hand over his thick, silver hair. "Council is putting some pressure on me to find out what the new building is going to look like. How soon do you think you can have a presentation ready? It doesn't have to be anything fancy, but the demolition is already scheduled, and next week we'll begin moving records and office space into temporary quarters. Once the site is cleared, we can begin construction."

Uncle Bob looked happy. Matt wished he could say the same for Eve. Twin vertical furrows appeared above her pixie nose.

"What demolition?" she asked.

"We've made arrangements for the old Hall to be imploded," Uncle Bob told her. "Then we'll build the new Hall on the same site."

The furrows deepened. "Imploded?"

"That's what's done when the demolition of a large building might damage its neighbors." Uncle Bob spelled it out as if he were speaking to a child, and not a person far more familiar with the construction industry than he was. Matt threw up mental hands. Not much wonder his uncle rubbed her the wrong way. He really was a moron.

"I know why it's used." Her pink-tipped toes tapped on the tiled floor. "But a new site has already been bought, and Sullivan Construction agreed to site preparation as part of the bid."

"It was agreed that the current property remains the best choice to build on because it's centrally located," Uncle Bob said. "Since the old building has already been decommissioned, we can bring it down and start over."

"You work fast," Eve said. "And quiet, too. I'll bet this bit of information hasn't hit the newspapers yet."

Uncle Bob beamed. "Thanks. It hasn't."

Matt wondered if his uncle realized she wasn't issuing him a compliment.

"Have you given any thought to how this is going to affect the budget?" she asked next. "You can't go around changing things without talking to Connor. He has a contract. Imploding the old building will cost a lot more than leveling off the property that was purchased for the new project."

Uncle Bob waved it off. "Connor and I are on the same page."

"You've already brought Matt into this. Now you want to change the building site. Do you have any idea how much implosion will add to site preparation costs?"

"Don't you go worrying about money," Uncle Bob said. "I have ways of covering additional expenses."

"It's my job to worry about money."

Matt noticed with increasing alarm that Eve was almost vibrating from the effort it took to control her frustration. For Uncle Bob's sake, Matt hoped he really did have ways of covering the additional expenses. He rubbed his leg, hoping that small gesture would be enough to cause a distraction and maybe win some sympathy. He wondered if a little moan would be overkill.

"I think I should lie down," he said.

At once, Eve turned all her attention to him.

"Sure. You go lie down. There's no big hurry on that design," Uncle Bob said cheerfully, reaching for the door. "It can wait a day or so until you're feeling better. Just don't let Evie sweet-talk you into drawing some low-budget eyesore." He disappeared with a wave of one hand.

Matt winced as he rose to his feet. *Low-budget eyesore.* There was no doubt about it. Uncle Bob seemed to go out of his way to antagonize Eve. The joke was on him, though. She wouldn't have to do much sweet-talking at all to get Matt to do just about anything she wanted at this point. He rubbed his leg again. Unfortunately, her methods of persuasion weren't what one could call "sweet."

"Here, let me help you." She wriggled her way under his arm as if she belonged there, and Matt's knees nearly buckled. Man, she was little. And strong. He'd been too drugged earlier to fully appreciate what it must have taken for her to get him in the house and up the stairs, but he knew he hadn't done it all alone. He dimly recalled her helping him out of his pants, too. Too bad he couldn't talk her into helping him take a shower.

The thought of being naked with her wasn't doing anything for his navigational skills as she helped him limp his way into the living room.

No, Uncle Bob, never in a million years would there be any reason other than business for me to be living with Eve.

Matt tried to come up with something to say to distract her from the flowers, the construction project, Uncle Bob, and the unwanted attention she was receiving from certain parts of his body.

"Thanks for showing such remarkable self-control with Uncle Bob," he said. "I know he can be hard to take sometimes, but he's important to me. All my life, he's stepped up to the plate whenever I've needed a dad. I owe him for that."

"How do you know I was using self-control?" she asked, the beginning of a smile tickling the corners of her curvy mouth.

He knew more about her than she might suspect. He probably knew more about her than she did herself. For instance, Eve shouldered way too much responsibility for work. And if she worried too much about work, she probably worried too much about other things in her life, too.

"I just do."

"Well, then, thank you for not saying anything to Bob about the real reason you moved in here."

This was the closest she'd come to discussing it with him, and he wanted to push, but didn't dare push too hard.

"How do you know I didn't?" Matt asked.

"I just do."

She said it with utter conviction, and a glimmer of pleasure lit Matt's insides. If she believed he'd never tell anyone her secrets, it meant she trusted him at least a little. And Matt discovered he would do a lot to earn Eve's trust. He liked her straightforwardness.

"I forgot to tell you," he said, stretching out on the sofa with his shoulders braced against one armrest, and both feet dangling off the other. "Your mother called last night. She and your father are coming for a visit at the end of the month."

He waited for her to bring up her house rules, especially the one about answering the phone, but she didn't. Instead, she adopted the air of a woman resigned to the inevitable.

Eve sighed. "My parents are planning this huge fortieth anniversary party. It's more of a family reunion. They're coming to the city to pick up things they can't buy in bulk locally. They always stay here. She'll never believe you're a roommate."

Matt was getting tired of her worrying that people might think there was something going on between them. He was considered quite a catch—by everyone but Eve.

Patience, he reminded himself. And lots of it. Let her come to him.

"I can move back into the hotel for a few days," he said, just to torment her. He'd probably go to Toronto, but he was curious how she planned to handle this before he gave her an out.

"At three hundred dollars a night?" She tightened the belt on her robe. "I don't think so. I'll sleep on the sofa. My parents will sleep in my bed."

"If anyone sleeps on the sofa, it should be me," Matt said. Then he wondered why he was offering to sleep on her sofa. It was two feet too short for him.

Eve measured him with her eyes, apparently coming to the same conclusion.

"We'll share your bedroom," she decided, looking less than enthusiastic but prepared to suffer. "I'll set up an air mattress on the floor for myself. It's either that or you stay with Bob."

As much as Matt liked the idea of sharing a room with her, he didn't think he could enjoy it with her parents a few feet away. Having lain awake at night listening to her sheets rustling when she moved and the small, breathy noises she made when she slept, he knew how thin the walls were.

"What will your parents think about you sharing your room with a man they've never met?" he asked, mostly because testing her problem-solving skills was proving entertaining.

"The same thing they'll think if you sleep on the sofa,

only that we're being more honest about it," she said. "There's nothing I can say to my mother that will convince her you're a roommate, so let her think what she wants. We might as well be comfortable. I'm not a teenager anymore. I quit worrying about what she thought a long time ago."

Which meant she really hadn't. Matt wondered what there was between Eve and her mother that made her so testy over the thought of such a short visit.

He wondered, too, who she thought was going to be comfortable with the sleeping arrangements she'd suggested, because it wouldn't be him. Judging by the expression on her face, it wouldn't be her, either.

No, sharing a room was out of the question. He'd definitely take that trip back to Toronto he'd been putting off, but he'd wait until after her parents arrived to tell her about it. Matt smiled to himself.

Let Eve spend the next two weeks worrying about having to share a bedroom with him. She'd been causing him plenty of sleepless nights already, and he anticipated more to come.

Chapter Eight

Eve rubbed her temples and stared out of her tiny office window overlooking the parking lot. Matt had dropped her off that morning, as he had every other day during the past two weeks when he'd needed to borrow her car, then gone home to wait for a delivery.

The meeting Bob had arranged with City Council was set for eleven o'clock, and Matt's drafting department in Toronto was sending the preliminary blueprints by priority post—for plans he wouldn't let her see beforehand, although he'd assured her over and over that he'd taken her notes into consideration and that she'd love the design.

He refused, however, to share it with her. She was willing to bet that it was because he wanted her to see the reaction of other people first before she started in with her list of complaints.

Maybe he was coming to know her a little too well.

If he'd truly taken her notes into consideration, then the least she could do was give his design a fair chance. But she wasn't going to get her hopes up. She was getting to know him better, too, and he had expensive tastes. His shampoo cost more than hers. Not that she had any right to judge how he spent his own money, but their ideas of fiscal restraint appeared to be vastly different. She wanted to get this meeting over with so she could get started on the budget.

Again.

To top it all off, her parents were due to arrive in the morning. There went her weekend.

The view of the parking lot didn't help the headache slamming behind her eyelids. She sat up straighter in her chair, all but pressing her nose against the pane of glass. Bob Anderson was getting out of a car. He was early, and that meant he was here to see someone beforehand. She prayed it wasn't going to be her.

The company secretary knocked on Eve's open door, nervously clearing her throat. "Hi. I thought I should tell you the site supervisor from out in Bedford called, and the delivery date for the structural steel you ordered has been moved back a week."

The day got better by the minute. Eve let out a long, slow breath. She had handed in a completed schedule for that particular project to Connor just that morning. Now she'd have to redo the whole thing.

She'd dressed for the office today, too. She kicked off her uncomfortable high heels and hung her thin, linen suit jacket over the back of a chair so it wouldn't wrinkle, then prepared to get back to work.

Bob's silvery head appeared in the doorway. "Hey, Evie. Got a minute?"

She wished she could break him of calling her that, but pointing it out made it worse. "What can I do for you?"

He cleared a stack of files from a spare chair crammed in a corner and drew it close to her desk. "Just thought I'd drop by early and invite everyone here at Sullivan Construction to a ground-breaking ceremony."

Eve's headache grew steadily worse. "You can't have a ground-breaking ceremony if you don't have any ground to break."

Bob dismissed that minor detail as if it were of no particular concern. "Then we'll make it another fundraising party and unveil the new plans to the public."

Eve pressed her fingertips against her eyebrows. "Shouldn't you wait until after the plans are approved?"

"They'll be approved." He picked up a stress ball from her desk and rolled it between his palms. "Matt's a great guy, you know. Shame he doesn't have a special someone in his life."

She thought she knew where this conversation was headed, and it had nothing to do with the upcoming meeting. "Don't even think about it. Matt's not my type."

"Of course he's not your type," Bob said, surprised. "You aren't his, either. Where would you even get such an idea? You two are all wrong for each other. Matt needs more of a… homebody."

There was an insult in there somewhere. Eve was sure of it.

"To knit him socks?" she suggested. "And fetch his slippers?"

"Ha ha." Bob thought about it. "But close. His dad died when Mattie was just a baby, and while I hate to say this about my own sister, his mother has always been kind of a flake. She didn't provide him with much affection growing up, yet he's such a low-key, gentle person himself. So responsible and reliable. While you, Evie…you're…" His voice trailed off as if he'd suddenly thought better of whatever it was he'd been about to say.

Eve's hands clenched into two tight fists. She rapped the back of her knuckles on the desktop. He'd better not be calling her a flake. "What am I?"

He flashed an apologetic smile. "You're kind of a bully."

Eve almost laughed. Almost, but not quite. Bob Anderson, who dwarfed her by almost a foot—who steamrolled over people like he was spreading hot asphalt—thought *she* was a bully?

Her eyes narrowed. Had he also implied that she somehow wasn't responsible and reliable?

"I'll have you know that I'm very good at my job," she said, seizing on the one insult she felt most able to rebut. "I'm as responsible and reliable as anyone else in this industry, and more so than most."

"I can't argue with you there," Bob agreed, propelling his chair back a few inches. "Except you could be a little more careful with a nail gun, I suppose."

Eve's mouth opened and closed.

Connor chose that split second of indecision to interrupt. "Bob! I thought I heard your voice. Got a few minutes for a coffee?"

Bob leaped to his feet, relief evident on his face. "You bet." He paused and half turned back to Eve. "Want to join us, Evie?"

She forced a smile to her numb lips. "I can't. I have a new project schedule to complete."

The two men fled. She listened to their voices echoing down the hallway. Then, she crumpled up a sheet of paper and fired it at the wall.

The secretary came back in and made a move to lay some more papers in front of Eve. "Here are the typed minutes you requested from the last project meeting."

"Do you think I'm a bully?" Eve demanded.

"Of course not." The secretary dropped the minutes like they'd grown teeth and snarled at her. "Gotta go."

Eve twirled an earring. She might not be a bully, but maybe her people skills could use some fine-tuning. She'd practice them at the meeting by being open-minded about the design.

As long as it wasn't some funky modern nightmare that would blow the budget out of the water, she could handle it.

...

The meeting was held in the air-conditioned boardroom at Sullivan Construction.

"Good afternoon." Connor breezed in behind Bob, and immediately got things underway by introducing everyone around the table. Aside from the Sullivan Construction team, the architect, and the mayor, there were three city councilors.

"Now," Connor said, taking his seat at the head of the table, "let's turn things over to Matt."

Eve couldn't take her eyes off him. She'd gotten used to the casual clothes he wore around home, but Matt donned a good suit like a second skin. The expensive cut underscored the long, lean muscles of his arms and legs, and the rich, fluid fabric flowed like water with every move he made. His cropped, tousled hair added a touch of untidiness that set him apart from the neatly combed councilors in the room, too. He looked confident, successful, and really, really sexy.

Eve's heart took an odd little tumble. Her heels pinched her toes, and her pantyhose itched at the waistband. She wore office attire only when she had to, and never looked that well put-together. Bob was right—she wasn't Matt's type at all. They were from different worlds.

Electric blue eyes connected briefly with hers in an intimate, almost-possessive display, intended solely for the benefit of the other males in the room.

There it was again, Eve thought, irritated. That way men had of marking territory, even when the territory didn't belong to them.

"*This is No-Man's Land, buddy*," she telegraphed. He smiled at her, then launched into his architect's spiel.

It was soon evident that Matt had, indeed, done his homework, just like he'd claimed.

"And," he concluded, stacking his notes together into a neat little pile, "since the preservation of the history of this region is an important factor, I took that into proper account."

He approached the drawings positioned at the front of the room and pulled back the cloth covering them, inviting everyone to come forward for a closer look.

Eve studied the blueprints with a combination of horror and resignation. It wasn't a funky modern nightmare at all. The building was beautiful. It was breathtaking. He'd taken her ideas and he'd made them...

Better. And she was a little jealous. But this building was so far out of their price range, she didn't know how to break it to people.

"It represents a ship, for the Atlantic Ocean," Matt explained to the room. "And the relationship this region has with the sea."

Eve leaned forward to review the blueprint. She smoothed the sheet with one fingertip, impressed and not wanting to be. "There isn't one straight line on the whole drawing. It would be impossible to build," she said.

"It's not impossible. We'll use a lattice-like grid steel structure to replace the concrete the engineers would normally use. Then we'll put local sandstone on the outside of the building to help it blend in with the neighbors."

"And where are you going to find the structural engineers who can build such a thing?" she asked. Not to mention that structural engineers didn't come any cheaper than architects.

"Your local technical college is on the cutting edge of this type of technology. One of the professors has been breaking new ground in free-standing steel structures. All the college needs is to have the same CAD program I use in my office, which they do. I checked."

Dollar signs continued to click before her eyes. Matt wasn't used to worrying about budgets, that much was obvious. "This is—"

"Innovative," Connor interrupted. He shot her a warning look. "We'll consult with the engineers and get a cost estimate. Then we can make a final decision."

"I like it." Bob, silent until now, added his two cents. "But do you suppose you could make it look more like a space ship? To represent the future?"

Space ship? Eve turned her head to stare.

Even Matt was startled by that suggestion. "I don't think a space ship would blend in well," he said cautiously. "Halifax isn't NASA."

"If we build this the way you've designed it, it will look like a ride at Disney World. Which would be so much better." Eve said it under her breath, but she knew Matt heard. Ripples of laughter meant others had heard, too. "But it's certainly modern," she added.

Matt's jaw set, the intimate, possessive look he'd given her earlier now gone from his eyes. She could tell by the glint of steel in them that she'd gone too far with the Disney remark.

"I could always stick a bit of gingerbread trim around the archways," he suggested. "Would that satisfy you?"

Now, he was just fighting dirty.

"Are they married?" she heard one councilor whisper to another. "Because they do a really good impression of it."

"I don't think they're married, but I hear they live

together," the second councilor whispered back.

Good news traveled fast.

"Putting up one more building with Palladian arches in this city would be cheating future populations," Matt continued. There were a few nods of agreement. "The past is important, yes, but so is the future. I believe my design encompasses both."

"And it's impressive." Connor rose from his seat, indicating that the meeting was over, and reached over to shake his hand. "I suggest we wait until we get the engineers' estimates before we discuss this any further."

The room was emptying fast, and Eve hustled to join the tail end of the queue.

Matt snagged the belt loop on the back of her skirt. "Not so fast."

He was beyond angry. The tiny jerk of muscle underneath his clean-shaven jaw gave that much away.

"I thought of everything—the history of the region, the other buildings bordering its location, even how much sun exposure the front entrance would receive—winter and summer. What's your real objection to my design?" His words were low and measured.

This couldn't be the first time someone hadn't fallen in love with one of his designs.

But she had. She simply couldn't bring herself to admit it. She'd convinced herself he couldn't come up with a terrific design, and she'd been wrong. On the other hand, she wasn't wrong about the cost. This building was never going to happen.

He clasped his hands together and tapped his lower lip with his index fingers. He raised an eyebrow and studied her for an excruciating moment. A sudden gleam erupted in his fierce blue eyes. He took two more steps toward her until her back was literally against the wall. He planted his palms on either side of her head and looked down at her.

"Do you know what I think?" he said. "I think you won't admit you like my design because you're afraid if you do, you'll be admitting you like me, too."

What?

He was so close that, if she leaned forward, she could press her cheek into the crisp, broad solidness of his white, cotton shirtfront. She could wrap her arms around him or rise up on her toes and kiss him on the corner of his solid, sexy mouth. She could breathe in his expensive, spicy aftershave, mint cough drops, and fabric softener, all mixed together in a heady male scent.

"It doesn't matter whether or not I like the design," Eve said over the sudden hammering of her heart. "Bottom line is that we can't afford it."

"So your only objection is the money?" Matt asked, shifting his body closer.

Eve struggled to remember what it was she was objecting to. He was standing far too near for her to think straight. His tie was temptingly close to her nose, and she grabbed the knot, giving it a hard tug, and he jerked back in surprise.

There. She could think again.

"I know how much money we're working with," she reminded him. "Bob would have to come up with a whole lot more in order to pay for your building, and I don't believe he can do it."

Matt took her fingers in his and held them against his chest. His hand was warm, strong, and swallowed hers whole. "You'd be amazed at what a person can do when given the proper incentive."

He might find himself somewhat amazed, too, if he kept this kind of incentive up. Eve found it difficult to figure him out sometimes. He enjoyed tormenting her—never going too far, just far enough to confuse her.

She heard footsteps in the corridor outside and remembered where they were. "Anyone could walk in here," she said, snatching her hand back. "This could prove embarrassing for the both of us."

"They already know we're living together." He slid his hands around her waist. "Tell me. If I got the extra money for the design, would you kiss me, Eve? And would you admit you liked it?"

She wasn't sure if he meant the kiss or the design, and she wasn't about to ask for clarification. She'd thought he was uptight and conservative when she'd first met him, but she might have to rethink that assessment since his fingers had edged their way beneath the hem of her jacket.

But Eve was nothing if not stubborn. Neither was she very good at Matt's brand of flirting, and she wasn't sure where they were drawing the line. She was calling his bluff. "If you want a kiss, come and get it."

He regarded her thoughtfully. "I don't think so," he finally said, and she felt the disappointment all the way down to her pinched toes in her office heels. He lifted his hand and ran a thumb across her lower lip. "How about…if you want a kiss, you ask me for it?"

The sound of a throat being cleared made both of them start.

"If I kiss you, will you buy me lunch?" Bob asked Matt from the doorway. "Because I need to talk to you. It's important." He shifted his steady gaze to Eve. "And Connor wants to see you in his office."

He left, closing the conference door behind him.

Matt looked at Eve. "If I have to buy him lunch, can I take it out of the budget?"

Eve grabbed his tie again and pulled his head down

where she could reach it, then planted a solid kiss square on his startled mouth.

He didn't stay startled for long. His tongue touched hers, nudging her lips farther apart. His hands slid deeper beneath the hem of her linen jacket. Eve burrowed in closer.

The kiss itself only lasted a few seconds. It took her longer to figure out where she was after it ended. His hands held her upright, and his mouth continued to hover a few inches from hers, his lips tipped in a smug smile.

All she'd intended was to prove she could resist him. She hadn't expected him to be such an enthusiastic participant. A line had been crossed, but she wasn't sure which one of them had gone over it.

She pried herself free. "Now Bob doesn't have to kiss you," she said, straightening Matt's tie and smoothing his shirt, trying to make light of what felt far from a light situation. "Unless you want him to, that is. In which case, you pay for lunch."

"This isn't over, Eve." Matt lowered his voice even though the door was now closed. "I left your car in the parking lot. I'll get Uncle Bob to drive me home later. He's got some meetings planned for the afternoon, but you've got my cell number. Call me if you need me."

Eve's hands were shaking as she tucked her blouse back into the waistband of her skirt. What she needed right now was a good, stiff drink—and her head examined, because she did like him. His design wasn't bad, either.

But she'd been fooled once before, and she didn't think she could stand it if Matt fooled her, too.

...

Matt guessed it would take two glasses of wine before his

uncle brought up the subject of Eve.

Uncle Bob always fortified himself before addressing anything controversial, although there was nothing he could say to ruin Matt's mood. Life was good. Eve couldn't kiss him like that and not feel anything for him.

He couldn't wait to get home. And when in the past thirty-odd years had he ever felt like that?

The waitress placed his meal in front of him and refilled his water glass. Matt had to admit to a certain amount of surprise that such a small city had a genuine Thai restaurant, with a menu that was limited but completely authentic and a full house. They'd had to wait to be served.

It was a bigger surprise to him that his meat-and-potatoes uncle would frequent it. The owner even knew him by name.

"I'm the mayor, Mattie. Everyone knows my name," his uncle said when Matt commented on it. "The city's not that big." He took another sip of his drink and regarded Matt with brooding eyes. "She's not your type, you know."

One and a half glasses. Uncle Bob must be in a hurry.

Matt took a bite of his spring roll, taking his own time. Delicious. The beef Pad Thai was good, too.

He didn't want to discuss Eve. His feelings for her—whatever those feelings might be—were private. He didn't even want to discuss them with her, let alone his uncle.

"I never said she was."

Uncle Bob looked relieved. "I'm glad you realize it. You're all wrong for her."

That threw him. "Why do you say that?"

"You've got to admit, Mattie." Uncle Bob rubbed the back of his neck and shrugged his shoulders. "You're a little too predictable. But Evie, on the other hand… Now, Evie's quite a woman."

Matt couldn't quite get his head around the conversation.

"I heard someone say you called her a bully."

"Oh, she is," Uncle Bob assured him. "About some things. When it comes to work, she'll pound you into the dirt. But she isn't dull, that's for sure. And she's a real little beauty, besides." He sighed, crumbling a piece of bread between his fingers, then got straight to the point. "She's never going to come around to your way of thinking."

Matt wasn't sure he understood. Were his feelings for Eve so transparent that even his uncle could read them? He liked her, more than liked her, and intended to explore what seemed to be a mutual interest, but he wasn't exactly ready to propose. Besides, Eve had baggage, and too much of it to haul around for the short while they were working together.

His fingers curled around his fork. "What's my 'way of thinking?'"

"About your design." Uncle Bob leaned forward, and Matt eased his grip on the cutlery. This wasn't going to be the conversation he'd feared. It was going to be worse.

"She'll sabotage it," he said, a dish crashing to the floor somewhere near the kitchen and punctuating his words. "I heard a rumor that if she can ensure a heritage-style building, she'll be invited by the province to bid for a spot on the art gallery restoration project slated for next year. Historic reconstruction and restoration is a specialty of hers."

Matt felt as if he'd been gut-kicked. All the air exploded from his lungs. That couldn't be true. Eve wouldn't get involved in politics, not even to further her career. She was too straightforward. No. Her only objection to his design was the price tag.

Because she didn't like to lose. It was obvious that Eve wasn't a very good sport.

"It's true," his uncle insisted, as if sensing Matt's disbelief. "The province and I have been fighting it out for over a year now, ever since we decided to go ahead and replace the old City Hall. Marion Balcom's been spearheading the project. They want to save the old building. Barring that, they want a heritage replication for the new one. You can never convince politicians that something might be out of their jurisdiction, though." Uncle Bob sounded tired. "They get a few tree-huggers and left-wing wackos protesting outside their doors, and they cave. It doesn't matter to them what the majority wants as long as the vocal minority gets off their backs."

"Correct me if I'm wrong, but aren't you one of those politicians?" Matt said. "How can you be so sure that you know what the majority of the people want?"

"I'm not saying the majority of the people want a modern City Hall. What they probably want is for us to fix up the old one while trying to save a few dollars." Uncle Bob rubbed his eyes, then picked up his drink again. "What I am saying is that people want a boost to the economy. Money talks. Look at this restaurant, Mattie." He waved an arm around him. "The first two years it was in business, it lost money because people were afraid to try something new. I found the owner some investors to keep him going because I hoped tourism would save it, plus bring in the locals. Now, it's a trendy hotspot. On weekends *I* can't even get a table without booking in advance.

"That's what I'm aiming for with this new City Hall, too. Your design will make it a tourist attraction. Hopefully it will spark a little controversy, then a lot of interest. Eventually, it will help move this province into the future.

"Don't get me wrong. I love the city the way it is." He downed the last of his drink. "But it has to grow—and I don't necessarily mean in size—if it wants to compete economically with other cities in this country. And I'll be damned if I let the province ruin things because of a vocal minority."

"You've got to be wrong about Eve's part in all this," Matt

said. He didn't care about minorities, leftists, or anyone else for that matter. Eve wouldn't try to change anyone's design for her own personal gain. Especially not one of his.

A passing waitress dropped a napkin, and Uncle Bob bent over to retrieve it for her. She smiled and thanked him before proceeding on her way, her pink skirt weaving through the crowd.

"Why are you telling me this, anyway?" Matt asked.

"Because Eve's a beautiful woman, and men do stupid things for beautiful women." Uncle Bob held up his hand when Matt would have interrupted. "You've already admitted you made concessions for her. I know your work, Mattie. I saw the concessions, too, and I can live with them. In fact, they're perfect for this city. You're an artist as much as you are an architect.

"But if you make any more concessions for Evie, you'll be compromising your own reputation. Not only that, but you'll be jeopardizing everything I've fought for, too. Right at this moment, City Council is uncommitted as to what kind of building they want, despite some outside pressure. They've left the decision up to me. For now. But it wouldn't take much to sway enough of them in another direction."

And Matt was expected to choose between his uncle's wishes and Eve's.

Right there, Matt lost his appetite. He owed his uncle for all the years he'd been there for him, when he'd taught Matt how to drive a car, or helped him out with college. Matt had never been made to feel obligated, and his uncle probably hadn't even considered that possibility when he'd asked for this favor, but the obligation was there just the same.

His uncle said his name, and not for the first time. Matt jumped. "Yes?"

"A word of advice." Uncle Bob waved a forkful of curried

chicken. "Whatever you end up doing, for God's sake, don't let her talk you into putting gingerbread trim on it."

...

Eve wasn't at home when Matt got there.

He gathered fliers that someone had crammed into the old mailbox still attached to the wall beside the front door. He went inside and shut off the alarm system, his good mood totally destroyed. First, Uncle Bob. Now Eve wasn't where she was supposed to be. It was as if they went out of their way to suck all the calm from his life.

He went to toss the fliers on the counter, then took a closer look. One of them seemed to be a page torn from a scientific journal.

He picked it up and scanned the article. It seemed a Dr. Claude LaPierre had been recently published on some shellfish research he'd completed. It was dry and almost incomprehensible to anyone not interested in the study.

Matt frowned. He could not, for the life of him, figure out what kind of message this was meant to convey. He sifted through the fliers to see what else might be hidden between them. He found a newspaper article in French from some local paper outside of Montreal, Quebec and guessed it was Claude's hometown by the glowing description of his life and work.

The accompanying photo was of more interest to Matt. He was curious what Eve had seen in the guy. The black-and-white image, although grainy, showed an average-looking man with thinning, blond hair and a wide smile.

Again Matt didn't understand the message, although it was obvious there was one. Since there was no threat in them however, and nothing to indicate it had even been Claude who had left them, he buried the papers inside a stack of newspapers waiting for recycling day. Eve didn't need to see them.

But now that Matt had a name and a little additional information, he thought he might make some quiet inquiries as to where Dr. Claude LaPierre, shellfish expert, was working these days.

The doorbell rang and Matt jumped. Maybe she'd forgotten her keys or how to disarm the new alarm system.

He hobbled to answer it. He'd spent the remainder of the day in a number of meetings, and his leg was stiff and sore from sitting for an extended period of time. He made a mental note to get up and move around more often.

It took him a few seconds to place the woman standing on the doorstep. When he did, his stomach plunged and his wariness soared. With the highs and lows his emotions were riding today, sooner or later he'd need medication.

"Hello, Matt." Lena Sullivan held up a pot and pushed her way past him before he could stop her. "I heard you had been injured, so I brought you some soup."

"That was very thoughtful of you." And a little weird, too. It had happened two weeks ago. Matt didn't quite know what to make of it.

"Eve's not here?" Lena asked, looking around.

"I'm not sure where she is or how long she'll be. I just got home myself." He didn't know what else to say. "Here, let me take that from you. I'll just put it in the kitchen."

Matt took the pot from Lena's hands. He headed down the hall and set it on the table. When he turned, he bumped into Lena, who was right behind him. "Sorry."

Lena wrapped her arms around his waist. "No problem."

Matt was seeing a very distinct problem. He tried to disengage himself, but she was stronger than he'd anticipated. "Mrs. Sullivan, I—"

"Call me Lena."

"Mrs. Sullivan." Matt eased her hands off his backside. "I'm thinking your husband might not like this."

Lena's full red lips crooked downward in a pout that was downright frightening. "Connor pays no attention to me."

Now Matt understood what was going on. Lena was the type of woman who, after finding herself married to an older man, worried whether or not she was still attractive to the rest of the male population. If he let on he found her attractive and flirted with her a little, sooner or later she'd give up.

"Connor must be crazy, then," he said. "You're a very beautiful woman."

She threw herself into his arms. Matt staggered backward. His hip struck the edge of the table, and the pot of soup slid a few sloppy inches. Then Lena attached herself to his lips, and he was too astonished to do more than grab her to steady himself.

She finally let him up for air, but Lena wasn't looking ready to back off. Instead, she was staring behind him. Her face warned Matt that things were about to become more awkward, not less. When he turned around to look, he wished he'd been prepared for exactly how awkward things would prove to be.

"We must have the wrong house."

The short, plump woman who spoke could only be Eve's mother. She had the same hair, although hers was streaked with gray, and the same chocolate-colored eyes. She even stared at Matt with the same cool expression Eve adopted when she was displeased.

It was obvious that Mrs. Doucette knew full well she wasn't in the wrong house. And the forbidding man behind her had to be Eve's father.

Chapter Nine

Lena recovered faster than Matt.

She slapped his face before spinning on her heel, her head held high as she brushed past Eve's parents.

Matt rubbed his stinging cheek, wishing that he could follow her and make as grand an exit. Sooner or later, however, he'd have to return.

He stared at the Doucettes. They stared back.

"You must be Eve's parents." He didn't bother offering to shake hands, although he did make a feeble attempt at a smile. But the rigid expressions on their faces didn't change, and his own smile tightened. "I'm Matt Brison, the architect for the new project Eve's working on." No response. What luck. Two more Doucettes who weren't impressed by his name. "You must have had a long drive." Although not nearly long enough, considering they were a day early. "Could I get you coffee or tea?" He dropped his hand to the top of the pot Lena had abandoned. "Or some soup?"

There was a definite chill in the air.

"No, thank you," Mrs. Doucette said.

Eve, toting bags of groceries, bounced into the kitchen. She'd changed from the skirt and heels she'd worn to the office into her usual jeans and a T-shirt, which meant she'd likely come straight home after work before going out again. That made him feel better—he'd been worried.

"I see you've met my parents," she said. "This is my mother, Therese, and my father, Giles. They arrived early, so we went out to pick up food for the weekend." She set the bags on the table, ignoring the tension in the room. "I ran into Lena on her way out. What did she want?"

If the sparkle in Eve's eyes was anything to judge by, she was enjoying this. And if so, Matt wasn't sharing her amusement. He doubted if there was anything he could say right now that would convince the senior Doucettes that he wasn't some sort of serial sex offender.

Nothing he could think of off the top of his head.

"She brought soup," Matt said.

Eve lifted the lid on the pot. "Mm. Turkey. Wasn't that nice of her? That's one less meal we'll have to worry about this weekend."

Yeah. Real nice. Lena was a thoughtful woman. Didn't Eve find it strange that her boss's wife was dropping off a pot of soup?

"Eve, could I speak with you in the living room, please?" Matt said. He transmitted a look meant to let her know it wasn't a request. "Now?"

Eve trailed him down the hall, and when they reached the living room, Matt slid the glass doors closed behind them. Where should he begin?

Just that afternoon, he'd had his hands—and his mouth—all over Eve. He'd spent the last several hours daydreaming about repeating the experience. He didn't want her parents to be the ones to tell her what they'd just seen. He didn't want her thinking he'd been touching another woman.

Okay, technically he had. But his intentions were good.

Maybe not medal-winning good…

Matt steadied himself. He'd just say it straight out and get it over with, then he'd try and explain how it happened. "When your parents walked in, Lena had her hands on my, uh, backside—and it might have looked like I was trying to kiss her."

"Wow," Eve said. "That's awful." Her eyes welled, and she put a hand over her mouth.

Although it made him feel kind of good to know she cared enough to be upset, the last thing he wanted was to make her cry. He shifted uneasily. "I can explain."

"Please." Her voice was muffled. She waved him off with her free hand. "There's no need to explain. I can picture it just fine."

She wasn't crying… She was laughing.

He felt his lips thin. He'd been caught in her house, with another woman in his arms, and she was *laughing* at him.

"Then would you mind explaining it to me?" he asked. "So I know we're both clear on what happened?"

"Lena knows I often work late on Fridays, so she made up an excuse to come over, hoping you'd be alone. She came on to you because that's what she does, and you tried to put her off without being mean about it. Because that's what you do." Eve smiled up at him, swiping her eyes with the heel of one hand. "Face it, Matt. You're too nice, sometimes."

Matt deflated like a beach ball with a slow leak. His uncle was right: he *was* boring. It seemed Eve thought so, too.

"Great. I'm a nice person. Could you tell your parents that?"

"They're going to believe what they want to believe. Don't worry about it." Eve looked ready to burst out laughing again at any moment.

Matt wasn't sharing the joke. A woman he wanted to be

naked with thought he was nice. That was the equivalent of "Let's be friends," and Matt didn't have too many friends he wanted to hear moaning his name—which was another thing he couldn't understand. Eve was none of the things he'd ever desired in a woman. She wasn't a leggy blonde. She wasn't the least bit domestic. She was far more interested in work than she was in him.

To top it off, now she thought he was *nice*.

Yet all she had to do was look up at him with those big brown eyes that sucked the breath right out of his body, and he'd do just about anything she asked. Ever since he'd gotten to know her, he was like putty in her hands.

Uncle Bob was right when he'd said men did stupid things for beautiful women. Eve was so beautiful it hurt to think all she might ever want from him was to be his friend.

"I'm sorry, Matt, but you deserved it. You're a bit of a flirt." Some of the laughter seeped from her lovely face. "I know you don't find this—"

"You don't know anything," he interrupted. He wasn't a flirt. Not with anyone else. So, she'd had a bad marriage. While she still had some issues regarding that, and her ex-husband didn't seem ready to let go, Eve had to move on. He'd been patient and understanding. It was time to get serious.

He hooked the front pocket of her hip-hugging jeans with a finger and drew her close until she was tight against him. She felt soft, not skinny as he'd first thought, and curvy in all the right places. His hand skimmed up her back until his fingers tangled in her mass of dark curls. It was time she realized exactly what his intentions were, and his intentions didn't include anything so dull as friendship.

With one hand cradling her head and an arm twined firmly around her waist, Matt took her lips with his—and he didn't try to be the least bit friendly about it. Instead, he tasted her with his tongue and his hands. The soft fabric of her T-shirt parted ways with the crisp denim of her jeans. His fingers blazed across the soft swell of her hip, gliding around and upward to rest with proprietary ease beneath the warmth of her breast. He wanted more—to get her T-shirt off, to see as well as touch. He needed to feel her bare skin against his.

He needed Eve.

She made a soft, husky, arousing little noise in the back of her throat that scattered his senses. Then, her hands tackled the buttons of his shirt. He lifted her into his arms, and she wrapped her legs around him, fiercely kissing him back. He buried his face in the clean scent of her, all no-nonsense soap and a faint trace of vanilla.

She'd pried enough buttons undone to be able to get her hands inside his shirt, and for a moment, he thought his heart might stop. This was it. Matt was going to make love to her, right here on the sofa. He wasn't taking the time to get her upstairs. He'd never make it.

He stumbled slightly when he stooped to lay her on the cushions, his injured leg still too stiff for certain movements. As he did, he caught a shimmer of their reflections in the sliding doors.

Glass doors.

Dear Lord. Was he really about to make love to Eve on the sofa where her parents could see them? For all he knew, they might have walked by already.

That thought worked faster than a cold shower.

Eve had him by the gaping sides of his shirt, tugging him toward her. Her T-shirt had slid up to expose the flat lines of her belly, a belly he would have given a kidney to be able to lean forward and press a kiss against. *Bad, bad idea.*

She was rumpled, but at least she was still decent. Another minute and she wouldn't have been. *Thank you, God, for small favors.*

"I'm sorry," he said, easing her shirt down inch by excruciating inch. She had no idea how sorry he was—the last thing he wanted to do right now was stop.

Correction. The last thing he wanted to do was embarrass her. The next time they reached this point, he'd make sure they were alone.

"Sorry?" Her eyes were wide and confused, like she'd been startled from a deep sleep. Or interrupted in the middle of making love. She had beautiful eyes. Deep, dark, *make love to me* eyes.

Matt fastened his shirt, his fingers fumbling with the uncooperative buttons. "Your parents are here," he reminded her. He had enough of an ego to be pleased he'd made her forget about them, but he was intensely glad they hadn't seen what he was trying to do to their daughter. He hoped. "They already think I'm a sex-crazed maniac. There's no need to confirm their opinion." He took her hand and tugged her to her feet. "I'd better spend the night at my uncle's."

She had no idea why he'd want to spend the night at his uncle's.

Neither could she make sense of what was going on. One minute she'd been laughing at the thought of Matt aggressively pursuing Lena, and the next she was flat on her back on the sofa.

"I'm the one who should be sorry," she said. For the second time that day, she'd pushed him too far. She tucked her T-shirt back in her jeans and struggled to find the right words to explain. "I'm a little too proactive."

And with her parents in the next room, too.

He looked startled, then ran his hands through his dusky

hair, his nearly translucent blue eyes crinkling at the corners. "Proactive is good. Really good."

That made her laugh, and just like that, her embarrassment faded. It made her like him a little bit more than she already did.

"You really are a nice person, Matt Brison," she said, reaching up to touch his cheek.

He caught her hand in his and pressed a kiss to her palm. Then he pulled her closer again. "Let's get one thing straight," he said. "The only reason I'm going to my uncle's tonight is because I refuse to get you naked with your parents in the house. Tomorrow, I have to fly to Toronto for a few days." His hot, intense eyes scoured her in a way that left little doubt as to what he was thinking. "And when I come back, believe me, I'm going to prove to you that I am not a nice person. And Eve?"

Eve held her breath, wondering what was coming next.

He dipped his head and gave her a gentle kiss this time, instead of the hot, soul-searing one his eyes promised. "While I'm gone, please try to be careful. If you need me, just call. And if you can't reach me, then call my uncle. I know you don't like him a whole lot, but he'll look out for you for me." His eyes softened. "I'd really hate to have anything happen to you."

Eve's heart dissolved into a little puddle on the floor.

Something was happening to her already, although she wasn't sure she wanted to identify it. Identifying it would mean having to think about the future.

And Eve wasn't ready for that.

· · ·

The next morning, Eve took her parents to a party rental

agency so they could book tables, chairs, outdoor lighting, and a tent. After that, they went to lunch at a small restaurant in a nearby mall. The waitress handed them menus, told them the specials, then wrote her name on a sheet of brown paper with a crayon.

Eve wondered when they would bring up the subject of Matt. She knew it was coming, and she'd bet odds of ten-to-one that her mother would start the proceedings.

They placed their orders and talked about the weather until their food arrived. One of her cousins had joined the army. A great-uncle in Ontario she'd never met had passed away.

Her father spread butter on a roll.

"About your houseguest…" Her mother's words trailed off, letting Eve know what she thought of the houseguest in question.

There it was. She loved her mother, but while they might share genes, in terms of personality they were poles apart—and Eve always felt hers came up short. She wasn't traditional enough for her dainty, Acadian French mother.

She plunged her fork into her salad. "What about him?"

Her mother fingered her napkin. "He seems to have a fondness for women."

"He can be as fond of them as he likes." Eve shrugged, feeling a tiny pang. "We're colleagues." Another pang. "He's renting a room from me while we work on a project. When the project ends, he'll head back to Toronto." And since she doubted if Halifax would ever need another Matt Brison building, it was unlikely their paths would cross again. *Pang, pang, pang.*

Her mother didn't appear convinced. "You have a history of getting involved with men, then changing your mind. And I'm concerned about the choices you make."

Whenever her mother was displeased with her, she alluded to Eve's ill-fated marriage.

"For the thousandth time"—Eve blew out a breath of frustration—"Claude wanted to head off to an island in the South Pacific and study the life-cycle of some rare breed of shellfish. I didn't want to live on an island without indoor plumbing or a doctor. We had different goals. I realized it too late."

"Claude was a nice man."

If her mother only knew. She dragged a home-cut french fry through a puddle of ketchup. "Trust me, Matt's a much nicer man."

Her mother's eyebrows rose a notch, and she looked down her nose at Eve, no mean feat for a tiny little woman. "I thought you were colleagues?"

"He's a *nice* colleague." Of course, he'd said he intended to prove to her he wasn't nice, and that he wanted to get her naked. Eve fidgeted in her seat. Her mother made her feel like a little girl. Matt made her feel like a woman. And Eve wasn't ready for any of this. "Do you have a point you're trying to make?" she asked.

Her mother folded her napkin and laid it beside her plate. "We'd love to see you settle down, but with the right man this time. We're concerned you're about to make another bad choice."

Eve wasn't about to make a bad choice, because she wasn't going to make a choice at all. She and Matt weren't involved in any permanent sense. Theirs would be a short-term arrangement, if anything. They both knew that. Eve took a sip of water. There wouldn't be any long-term commitment for her parents, or anyone else, to worry about.

"I'm almost thirty years old. I can make whatever choices I want," she said. "Besides, I won't be 'settling down' with Matt. Our relationship is a working one." How much plainer could she make it?

Eve's father spoke up. "I didn't like him."

Indignation on Matt's behalf pricked Eve. How could her father make such a snap decision? What wasn't to like?

"You don't know what you're talking about," she said, thumping her glass on the table. "Matt's a wonderful person." She warmed to her topic. "He's thoughtful and kind and generous. If you're basing your judgment on what you thought you saw last night, you're dead wrong. He was too polite to tell my boss's wife to leave him alone because he didn't want to hurt her feelings. And he's not involved with her, either," she added for good measure. What century were her parents raised in, anyway? Didn't they know that a woman could be… proactive?

What a great word. It covered a lot of territory.

"That woman was your boss's wife?" Her mother's horrified expression gave Eve the uneasy feeling she'd just buried Matt's good name instead of clearing it. This was why she normally never bothered explaining anything to her. Explanations only ever made things worse.

Her father, usually the quiet one and without too much to say, gave Eve an odd, speculative look.

"I was referring to Claude."

Eve slumped in her seat. She knew that look. Now her father thought she wanted Matt.

Unfortunately, her father was right.

· · ·

Matt snapped his laptop shut and looked around the crowded airport lounge.

Fogged in. Totally socked. He'd known when he'd hired the cab from the city that he was wasting his time going to the airport, but the thought of spending another night with his uncle, listening to conspiracy theories about Eve, was too much. Why couldn't his uncle see that, with her blunt opinions, she wasn't cut out for intrigue?

Spending the night at Halifax International Airport wasn't appealing, either, though. Matt really only had two options: he could head back to the city and try and find a hotel room, or he could stay at the airport hotel along with hundreds of other stranded, testy passengers.

But he missed Eve and was itching to call her, wanting to hear her voice.

Wanting her.

He checked the time. It was getting late. Why should he wait around the airport for the fog to lift, or head over to some lonely hotel room, when he could sneak back to Eve's house and sleep on her floor—okay, he was hoping in her bed, but he'd let her make the call on that—and be gone in the morning before her parents even knew he'd been there?

He just wanted to be with her, to make sure she was safe.

Matt gathered his belongings and went in search of a cab.

He tried to be as quiet as possible as he let himself in and disengaged the alarm system. So far, so good. Everyone seemed to be asleep.

He tiptoed up the stairs and knocked on the bedroom door, firmly but not too loud, listening hard. He didn't want to wake her parents.

Nothing.

He had to admit, the whole situation was a bit of a turn-on. He hadn't been the type of teenager to sneak around and get into trouble when he was growing up. He'd spent all his time getting good grades so he'd get into the best schools.

Yes, Matt guessed he really was boring. But things were about to change.

He eased the bedroom door shut behind him. The room was in complete darkness. She must have pulled the shades, because not even the streetlights from outside filtered through. He stumbled to the bed and reached down to give her shoulder a shake, remembering how hard she could be to waken.

"Eve," he whispered.

The softness his hand encountered told him immediately that this wasn't a shoulder he was shaking. Before he knew what was happening, a fist connected with his eye. Pain exploded around his cheek and nose. He staggered back, swearing. "What the hell's the matter with you?"

The light flickered on, and two people stared up at him from the bed. Eve's mother flapped her hand as if her fingers stung. Matt opened his mouth, then shut it again. What could he possibly say to explain this?

Eve's father was the one who finally broke the silence.

"How was Toronto?" he asked.

...

"I told you," Eve said. "My parents like my mattress better. My mother worries about Dad's back."

She doubted if Matt would appreciate her bursting out laughing, so the less said on the matter the better. Besides, she had a certain amount of sympathy for him. Her mother was tough. All five feet of her.

Matt straddled a kitchen chair and rested his chin on its high back while she stood between his knees and applied an ice pack to his swelling eye. The soft glow from the light over the kitchen sink created long shadows on the ceramic tiles and into the far corners of the room.

She held the pack in one hand and cupped the back of his head with the other. She wanted to curl her fingers into the thickness of his hair, to plant kisses along the hard edge of his cheek.

She concentrated on the ice pack instead. "How come you came home so early? I thought you'd be gone for a few days."

"Fog. And I wasn't trying to grope your mother," he added.

"I never said you were."

"I wasn't trying to grope you, either."

"I never even considered the possibility."

"You're awfully calm about this." He glared up at her with his good eye. Eve smiled back.

"Welcome to my world," she said, thinking how appealing he was when he was upset. "With three brothers, people were sneaking in and out of our house at all hours." She didn't add that she'd been the worst offender. "My parents are used to it."

"Are they used to someone touching your mother's... um..."

"That's a new one," Eve admitted, biting her lip. She wished she could have seen it. Matt — of all people — sneaking into her parents' bedroom in the dark and touching her mother's breast. He'd need therapy to recover from this.

He took the ice pack from her hand. "You seem to be enjoying this more than you should."

She grabbed it back and leaned forward, reapplying it to his eye. Matt might pretend to be all business, but inside, he was really very sensitive. She wanted to wrap her arms around him.

There was nothing to stop her. He'd had a bad day, and she could sympathize with that. She'd had her fair share of days where she could have used someone to lean on, and so far, Matt hadn't hesitated to lend her his support when he could.

She tossed the ice pack onto the table and slid her arms around his neck. He burrowed his head beneath her chin, the warmth of his breath spreading through the flimsy fabric of her nightdress, and she rubbed her cheek against his hair. He said nothing at first, seeming content just to feel her breathe, then sighed as he traced light circles on her hips with his thumbs, smoothing the thin fabric of her nightgown between his fingers.

Yes, Eve wanted him, and funny, wanting him didn't seem quite so scary when he touched her this way.

"I'd hoped your parents might like me," he said.

He shouldn't have to care what her parents thought. The conversation had the potential for becoming too serious, and Eve didn't want serious.

"At least you and my mother are getting to know each other better," she joked, trying to keep things light.

"Very funny."

Kneeling down in front of him and taking his face with its stubbly five-o'clock shadow between her hands, she looked him straight in his blue, blue eyes. Well, one blue eye. The other one was swollen and red.

"You might as well know now. My parents are never going to like you," she told him. "That's why I do. And I'm not afraid to admit it."

She gave him a light kiss, intending it to be funny, but something fell flat. The truth was, she liked Matt too much. The kind of *too much* that made her worry things might change, and that she was in danger of having too much of a good thing.

Matt laughed, sighed, then caught her lips with a feathery touch from his own. His hands stroked her forearms. "Wow. I've never been the boy a girl's parents objected to before."

"Stick with me, baby," Eve said, "and I can make you

objectionable to everyone you know." She'd meant that to be funny, too, but she really wasn't very good at diplomacy. She said what she meant, often without thinking, and she didn't see herself fitting easily into Matt's circle of acquaintances because of it.

She needed to relax. It wasn't as if she and Matt had to decide where they'd spend Christmas. They could enjoy each other for the next few months—maybe—and if one of them got tired before the project ended, Matt could always move back into a hotel.

His fingers tightened on her arms, and she saw the pulse leap on the underside of his jaw. His throat worked, his eyes never leaving her face. "You have no idea how much I want you."

"Oh, I think I do," she said.

She kissed him then, with all the desire she could pour into it, touching her tongue to his lips, parting them, exploring deeper, until they both were fighting for air. He tasted like coffee and mint chocolate.

He drew back, looking stunned, then took her waist in both hands and lifted her onto his knee. She flung an arm around his neck and held on, gripping the front of his shirt with her free hand.

"Matt! Your leg."

"My leg is fine." He held her chin. "Thank you, Eve."

Before she could ask him what for, he took her mouth in another kiss that could best be described as *hungry*. Heat blossomed and spread throughout her body. She clung to him, dimly aware that one of his hands had slipped past the hem of her nightgown and that she sat, nearly naked, on his lap.

This was a bad idea. Her parents were upstairs, probably wide-awake and waiting for her to come back to bed.

So what if they were? She was an adult, and this was her

home. Still, maybe she and Matt should consider moving this behind closed doors.

She caught hold of his wrists but didn't try and break the kiss. Matt did that all on his own.

"Don't tell me. Your parents." His expression was rueful as he glanced upward. He kissed her again, briefly, then let her go with a great show of reluctance. "I'll sleep on the sofa."

"You'll sleep in your own room, but it wouldn't hurt you to share your bed," Eve said. "I don't snore."

He half laughed, half groaned. "Don't do this to me," he said. "I want to do things right."

"I thought you were doing everything right already," she replied. "I don't think you can get it any more right."

"I don't want to start off with your parents hating me. If I sleep on the sofa, they might warm up to me eventually."

A cold feeling washed over her. That sounded ominous, like he planned on being around for a while. But anything beyond the present was more of a commitment than she was prepared to make. She wanted to be clear on that. People changed when they became too committed. She didn't want him to think he had a right to tell her what to do, or think, or wear. She didn't want him to change. She liked him the way he was.

And she didn't want anyone trying to change her.

"They won't need to warm up to you," she said as gently as she could, considering it was hard to be gentle when her stomach was waging a raging battle with panic. She tried to stand up, to put some distance between herself and Matt, but he gripped her thigh. He wasn't laughing anymore.

"What's that supposed to mean?"

She pried his fingers off her leg and stood up. Matt stood, too, towering over her and making her more nervous. She wet her lips. Why did she feel like she was about to suggest something he wasn't going to like?

"It means, if we're to keep things casual, we shouldn't plan on getting too friendly with each other's families. It would complicate things too much."

"I see," Matt said. His face went stony in the dim light. "Casual."

The refrigerator hummed quietly behind her.

"I don't do commitment very well." Eve tried hard not to be embarrassed at having to explain something so obvious.

For a moment, Matt said nothing.

"Has it ever occurred to you," he finally said, picking up the ice pack from the table and dropping it into the sink where it landed with a wet, squishy thud, "to stop and think that maybe your lousy marriage wasn't your fault?"

About a million times.

"Of course, it wasn't completely my fault," she said. "But it takes two people to make a marriage, and neither one of us held up our end."

This was it. She braced herself. He was going to tell her to forget it. She could handle the rejection, but she wished she hadn't been quite so open about what she was offering. She'd asked him to share his bed with her. How subtle was that?

"Okay," Matt said.

Oh, no. What had she done?

"Are you sure?" she asked, then cursed herself for being stupid enough to ask for confirmation. This was what she wanted, wasn't it? Why would she give him an opportunity to change his mind? Part of her hoped he'd back out, because another part of her began to get scared.

"I'm sure." He leaned over her and placed a kiss on the top of her head. "We'll do casual, Eve, if that's what you really want. But," he added, "you're going to have to romance me for it."

Chapter Ten

Matt couldn't be serious.

"You mean, as in flowers and candy?" she asked, her voice cracking a bit more than she liked.

Humor crept into his one functioning eye. "Oh, I don't think so. I've seen your opinion of men giving you flowers. You can do better than that."

No, she couldn't. Didn't her failed marriage tell him anything about her and her romantic abilities?

"This is a joke, right?"

"Do I look like I'm joking to you?"

He definitely didn't look like he was joking. With the one closed eye, the rumpled clothes, and the fierce set to his lean face, he seemed perfectly serious.

Way too serious. Sort of a sexy serious.

"I'm not romancing you," she said.

"Why not?" he challenged her. "If a man wants a casual relationship with a woman, he's expected to figure out what she likes and romance her at least a little for it. If you want casual, why shouldn't you be expected to romance me?"

Now Eve was confused. Was he telling her he wasn't all that interested in her, so if she was interested in him, she'd have to do all the work?

"Forget it. Forget the whole thing." Eve wished she could, too.

"I think I'm starting to see your problem," Matt said. "Your marriage was a twisted relationship, that much is obvious—and no way would I ever suggest you should have stuck it out—but it affected you more than you want to let on. So now, when relationships get too difficult for you, you just walk away."

His gaze narrowed. "Well, guess what? I'm going to make this real easy for you. I'm yours if you want me, for however long you want me. But you have to make me feel special first. And that means romancing me." He started for the hall. "I'll be sleeping on the air mattress, and I'm setting it up in the living room. But where I sleep after this weekend is up to you."

...

An early morning mist hung low over the neighborhood on Monday. Up and down the street, doors opened and closed and cars started as people got ready for work. Eve reached down and yanked a patch of dew-slickened dandelion leaves from her lawn, pitched them underhand onto the driveway in the direction of the compost container, then wiped her hand on her jeans.

The two men were packing the car, chatting like friends.

Matt canceled the flight to Toronto and had spent his entire Sunday doing his best to win over her parents—and with amazing results. It hadn't taken them long to forget both Lena and the breast-grabbing incident.

Because Matt would never dream of walking away from anything difficult. He liked a challenge.

And her mother was certainly a challenge.

She stood beside Eve on the short concrete walkway leading from the steps to the street. They both searched for something to say.

"I like your young man," her mother said. "We didn't get off to the best start, but you were right. He's nice."

"He's not my young man."

"He could be."

"Didn't you have someone you wanted me to meet?" Eve asked, anxious to throw her mother off the scent. When it came to man-hunting for Eve, her mother morphed into a bloodhound.

Her mother smoothed her hair into place, then adjusted her starched white blouse. "I did. But he was no one special."

But at some point she'd thought him special enough for Eve. "You know, after thinking about it, I'm not one hundred percent sure Matt and Lena don't have something going on between them," Eve said. "It's a little odd my boss's wife would be over here when I'm not around, don't you think?"

"She's no competition for you, sweetheart. From what I saw, you're much prettier." Her mother looked her over carefully. "At least you would be if you fixed yourself up a little and maybe did something with your hair."

Mothers were the reason for the term "justifiable homicide." Eve cut her off before she could launch into any more self-improvement tips.

"Don't get your hopes up too high," she warned. "Matt's mother's been married five times, and I don't think it's made him view marriage very favorably." Not to mention, Eve wasn't thrilled with the institution herself.

"There's something to be said for living together," her ultra-traditional mother said. "You and Matt can take your time getting to know each other. You need to get to know

Matt's goals. That's what you said went wrong with Claude— you didn't really know what you both wanted in life."

"Matt and I aren't living together," Eve said, still trying to recover from the shock of hearing her mother—*her mother*—encouraging her to live with a man.

"Oh, no?" Her mother began to count on her fingers. "He cooked us breakfast. He has a key to your house. There are razor trimmings in your bathroom sink." She flashed a triumphant smile. "Call it what you will, but from where I stand, you two are living together."

Spots danced before Eve's eyes, and the world faded in and out for a moment. Fortunately, Matt and her father appeared on the front doorstep then, saving her from the conversation.

Matt, dressed in a suit for a day at the office, picked up her parents' suitcase and loped easily across the tiny front yard. He hoisted the suitcase into the car's open trunk.

Her heart did a crazy little tap dance. There was no doubt about it. She wanted him. But she wasn't sure to what extent. Her heart couldn't be trusted. It had been fooled before.

"And you'll be coming home with Eve for our anniversary party?" her father was saying to Matt as the two men shook hands good-bye.

Eve froze. She didn't want Matt to meet the rest of her family. Hadn't the Tinker Bell story suggested anything to him?

"Matt's a busy man," she interrupted. "He doesn't have the time to waste on a three-hour drive. That's three hours one way," she added for Matt's benefit.

"I think I can work it into my schedule." His eyes gleamed, and he shot her a look that dared her to argue with him.

No, no, no.

"It's not a formal party like you're used to. More of

a reunion. Most of the family is Acadian," she tried next, desperate to find something—anything—to make him change his mind. "A lot of them don't like speaking English."

"You'd be surprised what kinds of parties I've been to. And I speak French," Matt said.

Of course he did.

"My brothers will try and treat you like one of the family," she warned. "Trust me. You don't want that."

Instead of being put off, Matt seemed fascinated. "I've always wanted brothers. You've got, what—three?"

That answer pleased her parents as much as it worried Eve.

"You wouldn't want these ones," she said. Not if he wanted to live a long, healthy life. "They're kind of rough. You know, physical."

"It's an anniversary party, not mortal combat." Matt folded his arms across his chest, full of blissful, ignorant confidence. Eve pitied him.

Very well. He didn't know what he was setting himself up for, but he'd brought this on himself. He couldn't say she hadn't tried to warn him. At least one good thing would come from this. Once he'd met the whole family, a casual relationship was all he'd want to pursue with her.

She shrugged. "Suit yourself."

"Wonderful!" Her mother's face was beaming as she kissed Eve's cheek. "It will be nice to have you visit. Both of you. You can introduce Matt to the whole family. We'll see you on the weekend."

"Exactly how much family do you have?" Matt asked Eve.

Eve smiled. "You should have asked that question first."

She waved as her parents backed their car out of the drive, a funny little feeling in her throat. Spending a few days with them hadn't been as hard as she'd expected it to be, but it hadn't been wonderful, either. They disappeared around a corner, leaving her alone on the lawn with Matt.

And an empty house.

What she'd proposed in the darkness of night now seemed so...sordid in the bright light of day. She was such an idiot sometimes. How could they keep things casual when they were living together? How romantic could she be? How romantic did she want to be?

She plopped onto the steps, dropping her elbows to her knees and her head to her hands, suddenly unable to face the thought of entering that empty house with a man who made her forget everything but the way she felt. And the way she felt right now scared her. All she had to do was look at him in his custom-made suit, to smell his aftershave, to melt beneath those intense blue eyes, and she knew they weren't right for each other. When they were alone and he was kissing her... touching her...she could forget everything and everyone else. But when she tried to envision the two of them together, the way other people must see them...

What a contrast they must make. Eve's idea of dressing up for the office when there were no meetings scheduled meant she'd put on a stain-free blouse to go with her jeans and a pair of sandals instead of work boots. She studied her toes. She'd painted her nails Moroccan Plum. They looked nice, but they didn't exactly scream elegance.

"What's the matter?" Matt asked. He sat down beside her.

"I can't romance you," she said, glad she didn't have to look at him when she said it. "Sorry. But I can't think of a single romantic thing to do."

"I'm really not all that hard to please," he said. "It's the thought that counts. What do you think of when you think of romantic?"

He inched closer, but he didn't touch her. Eve wanted him to—and to touch him back. She wanted to lean into his chest, to find out if his fresh-shaven jaw was as smooth as it appeared, and to taste the swell of his full lower lip. She wished they weren't having this discussion on her front steps, with her neighbors waving to them as they left for work, when they themselves had to be at work in another twenty minutes or so.

But better to have it here, now, out in the open, rather than inside with too much privacy.

"I don't know," she said. "Handcuffs? Plastic wrap?"

She heard him swallow. Great. He was trying not to laugh at her.

"I'm not saying no. Those might prove interesting. But maybe we should work up to them." He gave her an all too brief hug, then a gentle shove. "We're going to be late for work if we don't get a move on."

"That reminds me," Eve said. "Where are the construction catalogs I brought home from the office?"

She swore she saw guilt on his face.

"Don't change the subject." He helped her to her feet, then looked into her eyes, softness and reassurance lurking in the deep ocean depths of his own. "Don't worry so much, Eve. You're going to figure out what's romantic when you're ready. And when you do, I'll be waiting."

Good thing Matt seemed like such a patient man, because Eve was afraid he was going to have a very long wait.

But if she waited too long, he'd be gone.

・・・

For the rest of the week, Matt carried around a vivid mental image of how Eve might look dressed in clear, clingy wrap. Each time he conjured up the image, he pictured himself slowly unwrapping her—from the bottom up, taking his time, touching and tasting each part he exposed.

The short, butter-yellow sundress she'd chosen to wear for the long car ride to her parents' house on Friday did nothing to hinder his fantasies.

Matt shifted in the passenger seat. So far, fantasies were all he had. Eve didn't seem to know the difference between sex and romance, but she was going to have to learn soon because the wait was killing him and time was now at a premium. He couldn't stay in Halifax forever.

Accepting the invitation to a family event because he'd wanted to tease her a little, and throw her off kilter, had been meant in good fun. He'd planned to back out at the last minute, using that preempted trip to Toronto as an excuse. But Eve had gotten quiet as the week went on, and he was learning to read the signs. This anniversary was important to her and he wanted it to go well. She needed moral support, but never in a million years would she ask for it.

He'd been informed of the basics for the weekend. Saturday was going to be a family day, more of a reunion than a formal party, with aunts, uncles, and cousins. Everyone but Eve lived in her parents' neighborhood, and Eve's brothers would arrive at the house in the morning to help out.

He had to confess, he was a little nervous about meeting them all at once. That Tinker Bell story implied a mob mentality that he hoped they'd outgrown.

"Is there anything I should know about your brothers before we arrive?" Matt asked.

"Have you ever played tackle soccer?"

"Is it like Australian football?"

"Sort of. But with fewer rules," Eve said. She reached

over and patted his knee. "But don't worry. I'll take good care of you."

"Thanks," Matt said.

It was early evening before they took the turn-off for the small village on the shore of the Bay of Fundy. The closer they got, however, the edgier she became. He worried that when they finally arrived he might have to pry her fingers off the steering wheel, which was ridiculous. She was lucky to have so much family to love her.

The temperature dropped several degrees as they left the highway. A few miles farther on, forests along the sides of the steadily climbing road gave way to giant rock slabs and scattered strands of scrubby, gnarled spruce trees stunted by the damp, salty air. Seagulls sailed high overhead.

They drove through a tiny village hugging the waterfront, then past a number of cottages sprinkled along the rock-ribbed cliffs. The gleaming blue waters of the Bay, peppered with whitecaps, dashed against the breakwater protecting the road.

Eve turned down a dirt lane. "This is it," she said, coasting the car through a deep rut and into a potholed driveway. "Home sweet home."

Home was a square, two-story house with a double-sloped, mansard-style roof and an attached garage. Matt bet the house, with its whitewashed, shingled siding and green trim, was around two-hundred years old, although the garage was probably only about fifty. There were one or two outbuildings, an ancient apple orchard, and a recently mowed hayfield behind the house.

She parked at the back and turned off the ignition, her fingers still on the key. "It's not too late to make a run for it." Then her parents stepped onto the sagging veranda, and a screen door flapped shut behind them. "Wait. Sorry. Yes, it is."

"I'm not running, Eve." Matt reached for the car door handle. He was no quitter. No matter what, he and Eve were going to have a good time this weekend. "I'm going to be right beside you."

"Come inside," Therese urged them once she'd hugged her daughter. "I have supper waiting for you."

They ate in the kitchen, seated at a sturdy table wrapped in a checkered vinyl tablecloth. Therese puttered between the table and the stove, chattering happily about the anniversary plans for the next day.

"We aren't going to need the tent," she said. "The weather's supposed to be lovely."

Partway through the meal, an ancient Great Dane plodded into the kitchen and settled beside Matt. The dog looked him straight in the eye, its graying, slobbery jowls quivering. Matt had read somewhere that dogs didn't like to make eye contact because it threatened them. He could only assume that either this dog hadn't read that particular book, or it was doing some serious threatening of its own.

"Riel likes you," Giles spoke up, mopping up the last of the gravy on his plate with a piece of bread.

Matt wished Riel liked him a little less. He was a big dog, and he made Matt feel like a great big doggie biscuit. Riel inched his nose closer, and Matt reached out to scratch his ears.

"Don't touch him," Therese warned, opening the back door. "He's arthritic. Touching him makes him cranky."

Matt yanked his fingers back. The dog bunched his creaky hips beneath himself and lumbered toward the open door when Therese called him, his toenails clicking against the chipped linoleum flooring.

Matt had to ask. "Why is the dog named Riel?"

"Eve named him after Louis Riel because he fights for

what he believes in. Mind you, what he believes in is his squeaky toy. Don't touch that, either." Giles set his fork on his plate with a satisfied sigh. "That was a good meal."

Matt looked at Eve. It made perfect sense to him that she would name her dog after the leader of a rebellion. "Your dog has a social conscience?"

Eve pushed her plate away, her own food scarcely touched. "Of course."

So far, those two words were the most she'd contributed to the dinner conversation.

He couldn't understand this attitude she had toward her family. When he was growing up, he'd been totally envious of friends with families like this. If she would only try a little harder, they'd meet her halfway. He was sure of it.

Maybe he could get the ball rolling.

"Eve's doing a great job on this new project," he said. "She's good with numbers, and the budget is a big responsibility."

"Thank you. Does this mean you'll rethink the marble inlay in the foyer?" Eve asked him.

He wiped his mouth on a paper napkin. "No."

"Eve's always been good with math," her mother said. "Too bad she failed English."

"I did not fail English," Eve said, tapping the end of her fork on the table. "I got a C for my final term mark in Grade Twelve."

"It kept her off the Honor Roll. Her brothers all made the Honor Roll."

This wasn't going as Matt intended. Time for a change in tactic. "I bet she was a cute baby."

Therese and Giles both laughed.

"You'd lose," Eve said.

"She had this funny head of hair that stood straight up on end no matter what I did to it. And she was all bones." Therese shook her head. "She looked like a skinned rabbit. I'd never seen such an ugly baby before. We were embarrassed to have her baptized. Would you like to see some pictures?"

"No," Eve said. "He wouldn't."

Actually, he was dying to see them, but he didn't dare say so. Not with Eve glaring at him that way. He gave up.

Therese began to clear off the table. "Why don't the pair of you take your tea out on the veranda?"

Matt tried not to cringe. He had his doubts about that tea. It had been steeping for a suspicious amount of time in a cast-iron kettle on the back burner of the stove.

Eve kicked him under the table and gathered up her plate. "We'll help with the dishes first."

"Right." He picked up his own plate and looked around for the dishwasher. There wasn't one. "Where do we put them?"

Therese took the plate from his hand and gave her daughter one of those long looks mothers give their children when they're displeased. "I'll wash the dishes. Matt's a guest."

"Matt doesn't mind." Eve turned to him, her chocolate eyes daring him to contradict her. "Do you, Matt?"

The last thing he wanted was to find himself in the middle of a mother-daughter dispute, especially between this particular pair. He looked to Giles for manly guidance. His desperation must have conveyed itself.

"Take the tea," Giles advised him, pushing away from the table and leaving his own dishes behind. He picked up the crossword puzzle and his reading glasses, and moved to a chair in a corner of the large room.

Matt took a deep breath, praying Giles had made the right call. "I'd love a cup of tea."

Eve filled two mugs with a wicked-looking brew, added a generous dose of canned milk to each, then handed one mug to Matt. She led the way onto the veranda, nudging him with a slender shoulder as the screen door swung shut with a *bang* behind them. "Wuss."

He took a tentative sip of his tea. It was strong, thick, and guaranteed to keep him awake all night. But not bad. He settled beside her on a patio swing at the far end of the veranda, rocking it gently with one foot. Fireflies flickered in the velvety darkness that blanketed the yard, and an owl hooted somewhere off in the distance.

"Mind telling me what I've done wrong?" he asked.

The soft scent of her hair tangled with the aroma of the tea. Matt loved her hair. His fingers always itched to touch it. He edged closer to her, and the swing squealed a protest. Even the furniture was against him tonight.

She gripped her mug in both hands and jerked her feet up, bringing her knees to chin level, forming a barrier between herself and the world. "I hate the way my mother always acts like a servant. You shouldn't encourage her."

That was it? He'd let her mother do as she pleased? And here he thought he'd done something terrible.

"Your mother doesn't act like any servant I've ever seen. She didn't want our help. She wanted us out of her kitchen."

"I know." Eve rolled her eyes. "She's such a housewife."

She said that like it was a bad thing. Matt didn't see what the problem was. As long as Therese enjoyed it, why should Eve complain?

"What's wrong with being a housewife?" he asked. "It's a job like any other, and your mother seems to take a great deal of pride in doing it well."

"Let her, then." Eve rested her chin on her knees. "But it's not for me. And that drives her crazy."

Matt took another sip of his tea and thought about that. "You're right. It's not for you," he said slowly. "And that drives you crazy, too, doesn't it?"

Eve tipped her head sideways, and his thoughts drifted to other, more pleasant things—like how the soft, exposed curve of her neck might taste by starlight. "You sound disappointed."

Matt gave the swing another push with his foot. His ideal woman had always been one who could make him a home, but not necessarily from scratch. Eve didn't possess any of the qualities he'd always thought he wanted in a life partner, except for the one thing that mattered to him the most.

She was Eve.

He admired her lovely face in the glow of the rising moon, debating whether or not to kiss her, but he'd already told her that she'd get to set the pace. If they sat here long enough, there was a good chance she might kiss him instead.

"You're a lot of things, but disappointing isn't one of them," he said. *Come on. There's moonlight, fresh salty air, and a cozy swing. Romantic enough. Kiss me.*

A large specter loomed from out of the shadows, then suddenly, Riel dropped his head on Matt's lap. Eve tried to shoo him away, but Riel refused to budge, and Matt reconciled himself to missing out on a kiss.

From Eve. Riel, on the other hand, was looking at him with adoration in those soulful, canine eyes.

"Okay, maybe I'm a little disappointed," Matt conceded. "But it's not because of you."

Chapter Eleven

Eve rolled over in the single, wrought-iron bed, the creaking of its springs and the sagging mattress tickling her awake. She could hear her mother downstairs in the kitchen.

Time to get up or she'd be late for school.

No, wait. Wrong decade.

She pried her lids all the way open and was greeted by the glassy stares of dozens of pairs of unblinking eyes. The bedroom walls were lined with shelves full of the many dolls her mother had given her over the years. Eve had always hated those dolls—along with all the frilly little dresses her mother used to make her wear. The harder her mother had tried to turn Eve into a girl, the more Eve wanted to be a boy.

Being a girl didn't seem so bad these days. She concentrated on the way Matt looked at her sometimes when he thought she wasn't watching—and even sometimes when he knew she was—and smiled. He made it plain he liked what he saw, and never gave the impression he thought there was room for improvement. And he'd seen her at her worst. Eve no longer thought Matt would turn out to be another Claude. If anything, he was the anti-Claude.

And that made him pretty close to perfect.

Eve wasn't sure she could deal with all that perfection. Getting more deeply involved with Matt wouldn't be any better for her self-esteem than Claude had been, because now she really was the one who had room for improvement.

And this time she cared. Which only meant one thing—he could hurt her an awful lot.

Plus, we work together, she reminded herself. She took a deep breath as she stared at a long crack in the ceiling. And once the job was over, their lives would go back to being incredibly different. She tried to imagine sitting down to Christmas dinner with Bob Anderson. Even better, she tried to imagine Bob sitting down to Christmas dinner with her brothers.

Then, she hoped that Matt lived through the day.

She'd better get up. There was a lot of work involved in entertaining the entire Doucette clan for a whole day of activities, and it was the best distraction she could ask for.

She dressed quickly and tried to be quiet on the stairs so as not to disturb Matt. She halted in surprise when she entered the kitchen.

"Hi." A warm smile lit his face when he greeted her. He had flour on his forehead and looked so adorable Eve's bare toes curled. He held up a mound of dough for her inspection. "Your mother is giving me a bread-making lesson. She says men make better bread than women because we're stronger."

He slapped the dough on the floured countertop and kneaded it with all the finesse of an expert.

Eve took a quick glance around the room to make sure they were alone, then dropped her voice to a whisper. "Only my mother would make bread on the morning she's hosting a huge anniversary party. She thinks she's Superwoman."

Matt paused in mid-motion. "I'll have you know that I'm making the bread. Does that make me Superman?"

"I don't know about Superman." Eve gave him a slow, playful inspection from his head to his toes. "But I do think a man in an apron is incredibly sexy."

Sunshine broke through the thick morning mist, streaming across the red-and-gray-tiled linoleum floor, and Matt's fingers stilled. "I guess we're both in luck, then. I think a woman in an apron happens to be sexy, too."

"That means I'm out. The only apron I own is for when I have a hammer and a bucket of nails."

Matt abandoned the bread dough, snagged her with floury fingers, and drew her to him, his hands large, warm, and steady. His eyes were bluer than the waters of the Bay, visible behind him through the tall kitchen window. "Those are the sexiest kind."

Whenever he smiled at her like that, her body went hot all over. He didn't seem to care that she wasn't domestic or that she hated frilly clothes. He liked her for who she was. She looped her arms around his neck and drew his head down for a kiss.

Matt rested his forehead against hers, his hands on her backside. "What was that for?"

She considered all the possible explanations. Because he looked so sexy all covered in flour. Because he'd told her she didn't disappoint him. Because he made her feel good.

But she couldn't very well tell him that she wanted him. Not in her mother's kitchen.

"It's an old Acadian custom to kiss the cook," she said.

"Then I'm all in favor of old Acadian customs." His freshly shaven jaw nuzzled the sensitive skin beneath her ear.

Footsteps sounded on the back porch, and they sprang away from each other. Rather, Eve sprang. Matt had to be pushed. He made a face at her before turning back to the neglected dough.

"Aren't you both the pair of early birds?" Her mother set the eggs she'd gathered into a basket beside the sink, then washed her hands.

Eve's face felt hot, like she'd been caught doing something naughty instead of just thinking about it.

"Why don't you let me finish the bread?" Eve suggested to Matt. "You're a guest, remember?"

She hoped he wouldn't remember that she'd wanted him to help wash dishes just the night before, and he'd still been a guest then. But last night they weren't expecting her brothers to arrive at any moment, and Matt didn't need them to see him looking so domestic.

"And let you get all the glory? Not a chance," he said. He gave the dough another slap. "Back off."

"Leave him alone," her mother said. "Men are good at bread-making."

Eve couldn't recall any time she'd ever seen a man making bread in this house before. "If that's true, how come none of the boys ever had to do it?"

"When was the last time you made bread?" her mother countered. "As I recall, you were never any good at it."

Okay, that round went to her mother.

Eve poured herself a cup of coffee from the pot on the stove and wandered over to the window while her mother supervised getting the bread dough into the pans. Every once in a while, she would cast Eve an odd look.

"Is it just me, or is my mother acting weird?" Eve asked Matt after her mother finally disappeared. "I mean, weirder than usual?"

"I think she was curious." His eyes danced. "You have two big, white handprints on the seat of your pants."

Again, her heart did that little pitter-pattery thing it always did when he smiled at her that way. She craned her neck, trying to see. "Lovely. I'd better change before people start to arrive."

Too late.

Her oldest brother, Cyril, burst into the kitchen. He wasn't anywhere near as tall as Matt, but he was rock solid—and all of it muscle. When he entered a room, people noticed. Right behind him were Marcel and Alain. Marcel wore his dark hair pulled back from his face and tied in a ponytail. Alain kept his hair short and neat, because he was slowly going bald. With their different styles, heavy shoulders, and thick necks, they looked like a professional tag team.

Alain grabbed her first.

"Eve!" he cried, swinging her off her feet before tossing her over his shoulder like he was planning to save her from a burning building. "We've missed you."

Eve winced, air hissing from her lungs. Her reflexes weren't what they used to be. She should have been better prepared for this.

Matt cleared his throat. Four heads, hers included, swiveled in his direction. Alain let Eve slide to her feet.

Matt stuck out a hand still sticky with traces of bread dough. "Hi. I'm Matt Brison. Eve and I work together."

The men all shook hands, which Eve took as a promising sign.

Then Marcel tipped his head sideways, eyeing the seat of Eve's pants. "Looks like maybe you play together, too."

That wasn't nearly as promising. Eve began babbling introductions to cover for it.

"Matt, this is Cyril, Marcel, and Alain. My brothers. Cyril's the self-defense instructor I told you about. Alain's in the Navy. And Marcel—believe it or not—works for the Royal Canadian Mounted Police." *So don't mess with them.*

Matt didn't seem impressed. Or as scared as he should be.

"You don't look like a carpenter," Alain said to him.

"I'm not. I'm an architect."

The men were all sizing each other up. Her brothers didn't seem impressed with Matt, either. And they definitely weren't feeling any fear.

Cyril rolled one meaty shoulder. "How about it, Matt? Do you like to play games? Because when all the family gets together like this, we usually play soccer."

If Eve didn't do something fast, Matt was a dead man.

"He's not playing soccer with us," she said hastily. "Matt brought his laptop with him so he can get some work done this weekend."

"Are you playing soccer?" Matt asked her.

Uh oh. "Yes," she admitted. She had her reputation in the family to maintain. "But I've played with them before. You haven't."

A stubborn look she'd never seen before crept into his eyes. This was it. She might as well kiss him good-bye.

"If you're playing, then so am I," he said.

Marcel slapped Matt on the back. "Welcome to the team. Why don't you wash off that flour, ditch the apron, and come give us a hand? We're setting up tables on the front lawn."

See, Eve? Matt's satisfied expression read as her brothers filed out the door. *Things are going great.*

Eve rose on her tiptoes and kissed him on the cheek.

"What's that for this time?" he asked, his expression softening again now that the Neanderthals were gone. "Not that I'm complaining, mind you. I'm just curious."

It was for thinking she needed protecting. For thinking he could take on her brothers. For not caring that he'd been wearing an apron around all that macho, male attitude.

"Because I'm going to miss your pretty face," she said. "Those guys are planning to kill you."

"Thanks for the vote of confidence." He untied the apron and slung it on a hook near the sink. "You know, Eve, you don't understand men nearly as well as you think you do."

And Eve didn't understand what this soccer match was really all about.

Yes, Matt knew her brothers planned to kick his ass, and yes, he also knew they thought he was a sissy because he was an architect and not something more manly, like a carpenter. But what none of them realized was that growing up a skinny, bookish kid with no father, a guy either learned to look after himself or got his butt kicked on a regular basis. These days, no one kicked Matt's butt unless he let them, and if getting along with Eve's family meant taking a few hits, then fine. A couple of bruises didn't bother him.

The warm afternoon sunshine toasted the back of his neck as everyone gathered to choose sides in the hayfield behind the house. Most of the women and children, and the older men, sat on scattered blankets in the shade around the apple trees to watch.

Eve hadn't been kidding when she'd hinted about the size of her family, he realized, awed. Once the aunts, uncles, cousins, and their spouses were all factored in, they had enough players for an entire league.

"I want Matt on my team," Eve said.

She'd tied her hair back in a long French braid, the tip curling over her shoulder against her breast. She tossed the braid impatiently out of her way, lithe and gorgeous in a pair of cutoffs that didn't quite cover everything when she bent over—and she did far too much bending for Matt's personal comfort. One or two cousins-by-marriage were doing a bit too much looking for his comfort, too.

"I don't think so," Cyril disagreed, calling Matt's reluctant attention back to the matter at hand. "I think we'd better put him on my team."

That came as a surprise. Matt would have thought the self-defense instructor would have wanted to be in a better position to hit him. It was hard to hit your own team member and make it look like an accident.

"Just so you know, we play to win," Alain said to Matt, elbowing him as the game began. "You have medical coverage, right? Because Eve's real competitive."

What was that supposed to mean?

It didn't take Matt long to figure it out, not when there was no referee and Eve's brothers kept feeding him the ball. They weren't just trying to kick his ass; they really were trying to get him killed—and apparently, Eve was their weapon of choice. Alain wasn't kidding when he'd said his sister was competitive. She seemed to be her team's enforcer.

Matt had to admire her brothers. They were a whole lot smarter than he'd given them credit for. He was about to get his ass handed to him by a girl, and in front of her entire family. If they hadn't thought him a sissy before, they were going to now.

Eve, however, wasn't cooperating. Every time someone sent Matt the ball she dropped back, refusing to challenge him. At first he was pleased she'd caught on and wasn't about to play her brothers' stupid game. Then he realized something.

She didn't play along because she didn't want to hurt him. And everybody watching knew it.

Matt could live with her whole family thinking he was a sissy architect, but there was no way he was having Eve think it, too. He took the ball down the side of the field. If she wouldn't challenge him, he'd find someone else to do it for her.

Someone hit him from behind. Hard.

"Are we playing Australian rules?" Matt asked, picking himself up and trying not to groan.

"Puh-lease," Eve said, rolling her eyes as she rushed over to make sure he was still breathing. "Have you noticed any rules?"

She bent down to examine him, her hands on her knees, and just as she was making a move to wipe the blood off a small scrape on her knee, Marcel checked her from behind.

Matt's heart stopped as she went down, but before he could come to her rescue, she'd snatched at the hair on Marcel's leg in retaliation.

"Ouch!" Marcel yelped, rubbing the newly acquired bald spot on the back of his calf. "You're getting slow in your old age, Eve. And mean."

Matt's heart started pounding again, this time with ill-contained anger. Dancing lightly on the balls of his feet, he made a move toward Marcel, but someone grabbed him by the arm to stop him. Matt whirled around, and Cyril's palm shot up in self-defense.

"Easy there, baker boy," Cyril murmured, stepping out of the range of Matt's longer reach. "Marcel's just trying to keep her tough. He's not going to hurt her. Watch."

With a sudden deft twist of her body, Eve had Marcel flat on his back, one knee on his chest, her other pressed into his throat. Matt peered down into Marcel's face from over Eve's shoulder.

"Was that tough enough for you?" Matt asked.

"Get off your brother, Eve," her mother called out from beneath a twisted apple tree where she'd been chatting with some relatives. "He's got a bad back."

"And lousy reflexes," Alain added in an aside to Matt,

apparently unaware that Matt wasn't seeing the humor. "Don't know what the RCMP sees in him if a woman can take him out like that. I think he's ready for a desk job."

Eve scrambled to her feet, pushing a strand of hair away from her flushed face.

"And I think Matt's ready for a break," Cyril said to Eve, although his watchful eyes remained on Matt. "Why don't we let someone else play for a while?"

"I don't need a break," Matt said.

Eve looked from her brother to Matt, suddenly seeming to notice that something was wrong.

"I need one," Eve said to Matt. "I could use something to drink. Why don't you join me?"

Her shirt was sticking to her skin, there were flecks of dirt and grass clinging to her legs, and her hair was a mess. Matt had never been so attracted to a woman in his life.

That was the trouble. His feelings for Eve were a whole lot more complicated than he'd bargained for. This caveman mentality—the primeval part of him that wanted to kill anyone who touched her—wasn't something he was comfortable with. He was used to being in control of both his life and his emotions, but since he'd met Eve, there had been nothing but chaos.

Maybe he'd better take that break after all. At the moment, he didn't feel much like letting anyone kick his butt. Not when he felt like kicking it himself.

Eve followed him off the field, and the soccer game resumed.

"What's wrong?" she asked him.

She really didn't know…

Matt took a couple of deep, steadying breaths. He hated losing his temper, and he hated her brothers for making him. But, more than anything, he was angry with himself. He'd almost decked her brother during a soccer game. As weird and twisted as the game was.

Matt had always wanted to be a part of a big, noisy family that gathered for anniversaries and organized things like soccer games, but this business of trying to kill each other was too crazy for him. Not much wonder she didn't know anything about romance. Look what she had for examples.

"Nothing's wrong," he said.

They stopped at the table with the drinks on it, then crossed to the blankets where Eve's mother was sitting.

Eve tried to lag behind, but Matt caught her fingers and pulled her with him. If she tried to get into that soccer game again, he was tossing her into the car and driving her straight back to the city.

"Come meet Eve's cousins," Therese welcomed him. "Isabel, Jeanne, this is Eve's boyfriend, Matt."

Eve made a strangling noise low in her throat, like she was choking on a breath mint or something equally small, as Matt shook hands with the women. The first was Jeanne, a pretty enough woman, although her face was too sharp for Matt's liking. She was married to the round-bellied man he'd seen earlier crushing a beer can on his forehead, the one who was now playing soccer but hanging back out of harm's way.

Smart man.

"I'm the architect on Eve's new project," Matt said, turning on the charm. The women in the family had to be better than the men.

"Dating the boss, are you?" Jeanne said to Eve.

Matt's charm slipped a notch. "You've got that backwards. I'm the one who's dating the boss." Eve's family already thought she could kick his butt, so what difference did it make if they thought she was his boss, too?

"We aren't dating," Eve said.

That did it. Matt was putting an end to Eve treating him like a stranger, especially in front of her family. They had an unusual relationship, true, but they were more than friends, and he was staking his claim, right here and now.

He slung his arm around her shoulders and kept it clamped in place so she couldn't shrug him off. "Technically speaking, no, we're not. We're living together."

One fossilized, gray-haired aunt raised lacquered eyebrows in evident disapproval. "Any possibility of marriage?"

Since that particular aunt seemed to be the mother of the woman whose husband had a fondness for beer cans and sleazy T-shirts, Matt didn't see what right she had to judge Eve's living arrangements.

"No," Eve said.

"It's just as well," the beer-can basher's wife said. "This way, you won't have to worry about whether or not to send back the wedding gifts."

The comment was more humorous than nasty, but the white marks around Eve's mouth told Matt she'd felt it, so he felt it, too. Didn't anyone in this family realize that her marriage had hurt her? Didn't any of them care that she wasn't as tough as they all—men and women included—seemed to think she was? She was only human.

"That's what I love most about Eve," he said. "She's more of a doer than a talker. She might not like admitting to them, but when she makes mistakes, she does something about it." Unlike Jeanne, who seemed content to hang in there with the beer-can crusher forever, although Matt wasn't sure she was the one who'd made the mistake in that relationship.

His eyes fastened on Eve's. "And she never makes the same one twice."

• • •

Sitting cross-legged on a blanket beside Matt, Eve laced a blade of grass through her fingers and tried not to be too charmed by his words of defense.

He'd meant well. She appreciated the effort. But thanks to his good intentions, her family was reading far too much into their relationship. Her cousins were probably already placing bets on how long the marriage would last.

"Matt lives in Toronto," she said. "He's renting a room from me until City Hall is finished." She smiled at Jeanne. "So we won't have to worry about returning wedding gifts."

"Really?" Jeanne said.

Eve wasn't sure she liked the speculation creeping into Jeanne's beady, off-center eyes. This was so like her cousin. Whatever Eve had, or did, Jeanne had to diminish it in some way.

At least the soccer game was wrapping up.

"Can I speak with you for a moment?" Matt said to Eve.

She wondered if she was in trouble. Sometimes it was hard to tell with him. "Can it wait?"

"No. It's business." He hauled her to her feet. "Excuse us, ladies."

"I don't think they're going off to pick out china patterns," Eve heard Jeanne murmur in satisfaction to Eve's aunt.

Matt marched Eve around the corner of the garage and trampled a fragrant patch of clover in his path. A swallow swooped under the garage eaves, disappearing into a crevice.

"Do you hate me?" he asked once they were safely out of earshot.

"Hate you?" she echoed. Her mind went blank. "Why would I hate you?"

"Because that's the only reason I can think of for why you're trying to sabotage me, here." He caught her chin in his hand so that she was forced to look at him. "Either that, or I think you're afraid that if they like me, you won't have any reason not to like me, too."

She concentrated on the fingertip-sized indent at the peak of his upper lip. His eyes dropped to her mouth, and she felt the tiny pulse below her jaw leap beneath his fingers, which were still cupping her chin. "I never said I didn't like you."

"Then name three things that you like about me," he challenged her. "Because I'm beginning to wonder if you hate all men or if it's just me. Not that I'd blame you if it's all of us," he added. "I've seen enough of your brothers to know why you'd feel that way. I just think it's something you should work on, and I'm willing to help you practice."

"You're crazy," Eve said. "I don't hate men. I work with men all the time. I certainly don't hate my brothers. And I don't hate you, either."

Matt smiled into her eyes. "Prove it. Three things."

"Are we talking physical, professional, or personal?" she hedged.

"Let's make it simple," he said. "One of each."

"Okay." Eve thought a moment. "Physical, then. Your nose."

"My *nose*?"

"You asked what I like. You didn't say I needed to explain it," Eve replied. "Professional," she continued. "I like your briefcase. And personal. I really like those navy blue boxer briefs you wear. Really."

"Let me get this straight," Matt said. "You like my nose, my briefcase, and my underwear? That's the best you can come up with?"

"Let's see you do better."

"Easily." Matt released her chin, then wrapped her snugly in his arms so that she had to tip her head back to look up at him. Her heart tripped a little faster. "I like the way your dark, sexy eyes light up whenever I walk into a room."

"They do not," Eve said. Although to be honest, she kind of liked the sound of *dark* and *sexy* when linked with her eyes.

"Quiet," he ordered, his arms tightening around her. "This is my fantasy."

"I'd like to file a protest. You never said we were allowed to fantasize. That's cheating."

"I'm about to cross your 'docile nature' off the 'personal' list," Matt warned.

"You have a *list*?"

"Of course. To continue…" He lowered his mouth and pressed a kiss to the soft swell of her throat. "I like the way you smell. Flowery. A little sweaty at the moment, but definitely still girly."

"Is my smell professional or personal?" Eve asked.

"I'm still on physical." He touched the tip of his tongue to her ear lobe. "And the way you taste. Mm. 'Sugar and spice and everything nice.' I like that, too."

Matt won. Hands down. But Eve wasn't about to tell him so until he was finished.

Unfortunately, he didn't get the chance. She heard one of her brothers calling his name, and she wriggled free from his arms.

"Excuse me." Cyril strode around the corner of the garage, holding up Matt's cell phone. "Oddly enough, it's for you."

"Thanks." Matt took the phone with a distinct lack of enthusiasm and walked toward the house, searching for a spot with better reception.

"You're a guy," Eve said to Cyril. "What would you find romantic?"

A pained expression cartwheeled across her brother's face. "Why ask me? Why not read a magazine or something?"

"That would be my preference, but since I don't have any handy, I'm stuck with you."

Cyril studied her. "You really like him, don't you?"

"Yes," she said with a sigh. "I really do." There was no point in denying it any longer. "A lot."

"Then try sharing something with him."

"You mean, like sex? Because that's what I'm trying to accomplish, here."

Cyril's face flushed a dull brick-red. "I figured that out already, and I don't need the details, thanks. But I meant, like a secret. A hope or a dream. Something you've never shared with anyone else." He stuck his hands in his shorts pockets. "Oh, yeah. And next time? You might want to let him flatten Marcel for you instead of doing it yourself."

"Matt would never flatten anyone," Eve said with absolute conviction. "He's too nice."

"If you say so," Cyril said, without any conviction at all. "But remember, there are other ways to flatten a guy than by hitting him. You might want to think about that, too."

Chapter Twelve

Matt's curiosity was piqued by the armload of blankets Eve was carrying to her car.

It was getting late, and the Doucette family reunion was finally winding down. He rested a shoulder against the weathered support of the veranda as the sounds of the few guests who remained inside the house drifted through the open windows into the still night air. He could hear the sounds of the Bay of Fundy not far off. City boy that he was—and a mainlander—to him it sounded like the static of a radio station gone off air.

"Need some help?" he asked Eve.

She waved him off without looking at him, although her cheeks reddened noticeably in the soft glow of the yard light. Her hair was long and loose, the way he liked it, curling down the slender line of her back. A corner of one blanket trailed in the dirt behind her.

Matt's heart trailed along with it. If she ever wanted him even a fraction as much as Matt wanted her, he'd consider himself a lucky man.

"I can manage." She tossed the blankets into the back of her car then looked up at him with a challenge in her pretty eyes. She fixed a hand on her hip. "Well? Are you coming or not?"

Whatever she was planning, it had something to do with him. Matt bit the inside of his cheek to hide his satisfaction. He loped down the steps, his long legs taking them two at a time.

"I wouldn't miss this."

The moon was bright and full and yellow, lighting their path as they drove down the narrow, winding dirt road that dipped from her parents' home to a deserted beach strewn with rocks and boulders. The waters of the bay stroked against the night sky—gleaming obsidian beneath black velvet.

Eve parked at the breakwater and turned off the engine. "The tide's out," she said. "Good thing, because I never thought to check the schedule."

"Does it make a difference?"

"Yes." She slanted a look at him. "The Bay of Fundy has the highest recorded tides in the world. When it's in, there isn't any beach. And it comes in fast." She opened her car door and took off her shoes. "Do you want to bring the blankets?"

Blankets, a beautiful woman, and a moonlit, deserted beach. All signs indicated he was being romanced. He crossed his fingers.

The night air was cool and fresh, and tasted like salt. Seals barked off in the distance. Matt took off his shoes and followed after Eve, the blankets bundled in his arms.

Skipping nimbly from rock to rock, she quickly outdistanced him. She wobbled once, and he held his breath until, with arms outstretched, she righted herself. It was so typical of her—to go running ahead without a thought for danger, not waiting to see if maybe he might like to hold her hand to make sure she was safe.

A large, flat boulder, tilted at one end like a table with two shortened legs, jutted out from the cliff wall. She clambered up, then turned to laugh at his slower progress as he picked his way carefully toward her by the pale light of the moon. A slight breeze lifted her hair.

Matt stopped to enjoy the sight of her. She looked so happy and carefree, and he wondered if he could design a house that would do justice to this image, and how he felt at this moment. Eve might not care for his art, but she knew how his mind worked because hers worked the same way. She'd understand the message he was trying to convey in the design.

It took him a second to figure out what that message was.

When he did, Matt closed his eyes and tried to start breathing again. He hadn't asked for this. He hadn't wanted it. He hadn't planned to fall in love with Eve…but he had. He hoped he wouldn't be stupid enough to blurt that out at the worst possible moment, because she clearly wasn't ready for it.

Eve might know how to say what was on her mind, but when it came to what she felt in her heart, actions spoke louder than words. Tonight was her message to him, a first step on her part, and he didn't want to do or say anything to frighten her off.

He paused below her, then handed up the blankets. The surf pounded behind them, while the wind sighed through the trees at the top of the cliff. She touched his cheek with one cold, wet toe.

"What are you thinking?" she asked.

That she looked like a siren in the moonlight, luring him onto the rocks and toward certain destruction.

But oh, baby, what a way to go.

Instead of answering her question, he hoisted his frame up beside her. The boulder was smooth beneath his hands and still warm from the day's heat. He wrapped a blanket around them both, then took her face in his palms. She closed her eyes, and he kissed them each in turn. The small breath she expelled was warm against his throat as desire washed over him.

His fingers trickled to the neck of her blouse and trembled, nearing the first button. He hesitated, waiting for a protest, but she made no sound. He slid the small, smooth orb from the fabric, then drifted on to the next one — and the next. A cloud skimmed across the moon, plunging their tiny world into a pool of inky darkness.

He had no idea what he should do next or what she might like. All he knew was what she didn't want, and what she didn't want was forever.

He told himself to go slow, to be careful not to scare her, not to leap on her and kiss every inch of her he could reach.

Not yet, anyway.

She stroked the backs of her fingers along the side of his cheek. He turned his head slightly and kissed her knuckles.

"You have an amazing face," she said, tracing his lips. "It's like one of your designs. All smooth curves over reinforced steel."

"You hate my designs."

"Not all of them," she said, with that touch of honesty he found so appealing. "And I do like your face."

"Especially my nose, right?"

"Among other things. You aren't the only one who can have a list."

He slipped his hands inside her shirt and against the warmth of her bare flesh, feeling the sudden leap of her heart. She clutched at him and drew him closer, the tip of her tongue tasting the V at the base of his neck. His own heart quickened.

"Do you want this, Eve?" He hated that he had to ask.

"Yes…I do." Her words were husky and laced with the

same desire that Matt himself fought so hard to control. He buried his face in her hair.

"Then ask me for it," he demanded softly. He knew she was afraid of commitment. He supposed that was to be expected, considering everything that had happened in her life. He didn't, however, want her to be afraid with him. Nor did he want to be the only one feeling something special. Was there a chance that Eve might learn to love him? Or was he foolish to think they might someday have more between them than the casual affair she claimed to want?

For what seemed like forever, there was silence. Then, her hands glided gently over him. "Let me show you."

"Not yet." Matt captured the corner of her soft mouth with a light touch from his own. "First, I have to hear you say it."

She drew back slightly, and he decided he was nuts to make her ask. What would he do if she refused?

"I want this, Matt…please." Her voice was low, steady, and certain against his chest.

The moon peeked out from behind the clouds, only to disappear again a few seconds later. The ice-cold fingers that had curled around his heart slowly eased their grip as she slipped her arms around his waist and held him tight.

They spread the blankets over the hard rock, then undressed slowly, punctuating their progress with little kisses in out-of-the-way places. Matt loved the feel of her. She was soft and silky, and melted into sighs when he touched her.

She rubbed the back of his leg with her foot, the rough friction only making him want her more. She trailed the tips of her fingers across his lips and jaw, then kissed his bare chest.

"Please," she begged, and Matt drew her on top of him, his hands on her hips as he guided them together.

He should be embarrassed by how ready he was for her,

but he'd waited too long and wanted her too much, and soon her cries of pleasure echoed with his.

...

They lay together for a long time afterward, listening to the sounds of the night and the beating of their hearts. Eve's was tripping along like a jackhammer.

Matt kissed the side of her neck, and her nerve endings sent out thousands of tiny electric impulses. Her shoulder jerked in response.

"You're ticklish." He said it as if it were some wondrous discovery. He wrapped his arms and the blanket more tightly around her, and rested his chin on the top of her head. "Are you cold?"

"No." How could she possibly be cold? She snuggled in deeper. It was nice having him fuss over her. Waves lapped against the rocks. "I used to come here a lot when I was a teenager," she said, trying to think of something about herself to share with him that wasn't physical. He said nothing, but she could tell he was listening. "I'd lie here and look at the stars and dream about what I was going to do with my life."

He stroked her back with long, gentle fingers, and she stretched, kitten-like, from her head to her toes.

"What things did you dream?"

She'd dreamed silly girl dreams. The kind where Prince Charming rode into town, declared his undying love, and whisked her away with him. Then Eve had discovered princes weren't always charming, undying love could be creepy, and that she didn't want to be whisked away. She wanted to walk on her own two feet.

"I can't remember," she said.

The stroke of his fingers turned into a gentle rub of the

palm of his hand. "Dreams are supposed to be about your heart's desire," he whispered against her hair.

"My heart doesn't have any desire."

"Hmm," he murmured.

She knew what was coming. She'd expected it long before this, but he wasn't the type of person to invade someone else's privacy without an invitation. By sleeping with him, she'd just given him one—gold-embossed, no less.

"Did your heart have desire when you were married?"

She didn't want to think about her marriage. She wanted to put it all behind her, and for five years, she'd tried to do just that. But Cyril had suggested she share something with Matt she'd never shared with anyone else, and this would have to be it. She drew her arms up between them and hugged herself, feeling naked on the inside as well as out.

"Claude's a marine biologist. I was so impressed with him when we first met. He was smart, and sweet, and said all the right things. I should have paid more attention to what he was doing, which was cutting me off from everyone I knew. I was a possession to him. He expected me to do whatever he said and got angry if I didn't. For a long time, I thought he knew best because he was so much smarter and better educated than me." She forced herself to be matter-of-fact. "The first time I really argued with him was when he wanted me to move to an island in the Pacific. He'd done all the paperwork without telling me, even took my passport. I said I wasn't going, and he raised a hand to hit me. I broke his nose and gave him two black eyes. And now I have the dubious distinction of being the only Doucette ever to have gotten a divorce. My family is very proud of me. Perhaps you can tell?"

"And you never told your family because your brothers would have killed him."

"Not really," Eve said. She was honest with him. "I didn't

want anyone to find out how big a mistake I'd really made. I felt stupid."

Matt rolled over on his side and pulled her with him, then kissed the tip of her nose. He stared down at her in the waning light of the moon. "Claude's not the only one out there who knows how to manipulate people who trust him. That doesn't make you stupid. And I don't think you'll hold your divorce-record distinction in the family forever. Not with those guys for brothers."

Eve laughed. And then, she knew. If she could have the one thing her heart desired at this very moment, it would be Matt's love. And if he gave her his, then she could give him hers. But never again was she going to offer something so valuable until she was sure she'd get it back.

"I'm sorry if tonight wasn't romantic enough for you," she said. "But this is the best I could do."

He ran his finger down the curve of her cheek. "It's better than enough." He pulled them both to a sitting position. "But I think right now, we're going to have to move to higher ground. My feet are getting wet."

"Your feet?" Eve grabbed his arm and tried to peer over the side of the boulder into the darkness beyond. Suddenly, the lapping of the waves sounded all too close. She stretched down her fingers and felt sprays of water, then frantically patted the rock around them.

"Matt? Where are our clothes?"

It was worth the loss of their clothes to hear her laughter, but next time — and Matt seriously hoped there would be a next time — he was going to make sure that nothing got knocked off their perch.

On the bright side, at least they still had the blankets.

"Hurry," she urged, preparing to slip into the black, frothy water. "We've got to get to the breakwater before the tide comes all the way in."

They picked their way over slippery rocks covered in sharp barnacles that scratched their feet. The icy saltwater itched Matt's skin and soon made his lower body go numb.

"This water's cold!" He didn't bother mentioning which part of him found it the coldest.

"Tell me about it," Eve said.

Matt could hear her teeth chattering. The water wasn't deep, but each wave submerged her to the waist before receding. She'd draped one of the blankets around her neck to try and keep it dry. He carried the other two around his own.

A slimy object wrapped around his ankle, something that normally wouldn't have bothered him, but in the darkness it was decidedly unsettling. He hoped it was seaweed.

He could see the breakwater outlined against the night sky, and just above it, moonlight glinting off the side of the car. He steadied her elbow, helping her stay upright against the determined tug of the undertow. "It's not much farther."

They reached the car without any serious missteps, thank goodness. All Matt could think about was getting Eve warm.

"Give me the keys," he said. "I'll start the car and crank the heater up for you."

She clutched a blanket around herself, shivering. "I don't have the keys. They were in my pocket."

And her pocket was in her shorts, which were probably half way to New Brunswick by now. He slumped against the car. Only Eve could have gotten them in this situation. He raised an eyebrow. And then he had to laugh. "Have you noticed that all our evenings together seem to end in some kind of disaster?"

"We still have our shoes." She pointed to them, neatly lined up beneath the car's bumper. "The moon is out, and it's only a twenty-minute walk."

A twenty-minute walk on a dirt road in the middle of the night, wearing nothing but sneakers and smiles. Matt again gave thanks for the blankets. "That's what I like about you, Eve. You're such a problem solver."

He rubbed her legs with a blanket to warm them before they started off, then insisted she wrap two of the blankets around herself.

Crickets chirped in the fields, and every once in a while, small animals could be heard rustling through the raspberry bushes along the side of the road. Eve, however, was much too quiet for Matt's liking. She wasn't already regretting the evening, was she?

How could she possibly regret it? As far as he was concerned, tonight was a win. He'd tried his best to be sensitive and not rush her to say things she might not be ready for, but he loved her so much his whole body throbbed with the force of it. He couldn't believe he was the only one feeling it. Maybe she just needed more time.

The minute he got her home to Halifax, he was going to find a way to show her that he loved her. He had a business to run, and he'd put off that trip to Toronto for far too long, but he needed her to understand that he planned to be there for her. One thought cheered him immensely: construction projects never ran on schedule.

They took a shortcut through a dew-soaked meadow of thigh-high timothy. By the time they reached the house, only the front light remained on. Eve and Matt kept to the shadows.

Matt looked down at his blanket-wrapped body. "How

are we supposed to get inside without anyone seeing us?"

"I've done this lots of times," Eve assured him. "We'll slip around the side of the house. I'll crawl up the trellis and in my bedroom window, then toss out some clothes for you. You can come in the front door."

On the surface there didn't seem to be any serious flaws with her plan—until she handed him her blanket. He tried to close his mouth. She was braver than he was. A little nudity didn't seem to bother her in the least. Matt wouldn't even consider the possibility of scaling that trellis with his bare backside—among other things—hanging out.

"You're climbing up *naked*?" he whispered.

"How do you expect me to hold on to a blanket?" she whispered back, preparing to hoist herself up.

Good point.

"Hurry up, then."

The trellis didn't look too sturdy as she climbed. Matt breathed a sigh of relief once she'd swung her legs over the windowsill and disappeared, then developed a sudden, uncomfortable itch between his shoulder blades. Someone was watching him. He heard a low growl and turned his head. Green eyes glowed in the shadows. *Riel*.

Last night, when Matt hadn't wanted his affection, Riel had slobbered him with doggie loving. Now he was growling. Talk about fickle.

"Nice boy." Matt put out his hand to pat him, then remembered that wasn't a good idea. He held his fingers low so Riel could smell them instead. "See? It's just me."

The dog ignored Matt's fingers with a regal sniff of disdain. He padded closer, and Matt could hear the crackle of arthritic joints. And faster than Matt would have thought possible considering the dog's age and infirmities, Riel snatched at the blanket.

A game of tug-of-war began.

"Let go, boy," Matt said softly, wishing Eve would hurry up with his clothes so he could let the dog have the stupid blanket. Riel growled louder in response.

Maybe if he let Riel have this blanket, Matt could wrap the other around himself instead. He let go just as an upstairs light flickered on.

Please let that be Eve.

Footsteps crunched in the gravel behind him, and the next thing he knew, a flashlight beam had caught him in its glare. Riel shook the blanket between his teeth, and Matt clutched the other in his arms.

"If you wanted to play with the dog, couldn't you at least have waited until morning?" Giles asked.

Matt had no response. He was too busy trying to cover as much of himself as possible. Riel gave one last, satisfied growl then backed away, grinning at Matt as if well pleased. Oh, yeah. Man's best friend.

Eve stuck her head out of the bedroom window, having taken the time to pull on her nightdress. Thank you, God. Now if only she'd keep quiet about what they'd been up to.

"I thought we'd agreed you wouldn't run naked around the neighborhood anymore," she called down.

On second thought, he'd much rather she'd told her father what they'd been up to.

In detail.

Giles slapped the flashlight into Matt's hand. "You might need this if that's what you have in mind," he said. "The nearest neighbor is two kilometers away." He walked off, calling for the dog to follow him.

Matt shone the light up at Eve, loving the mischief romping in her eyes despite the acute embarrassment she'd caused. "Thanks. You were a big help."

"Don't mention it," she said.

...

"But what I still don't understand is what happened to his clothes?"

"They got caught in the tide," Eve said to her mother.

"That doesn't make any sense." Therese watched as Eve packed her suitcase. "Couldn't he figure out for himself that it's too cold and rocky to swim, especially at night? Even if he couldn't, why wouldn't he leave his clothes higher up on the beach? And why didn't he think to check the car for the keys before walking home in the dark?"

Eve wondered what Matt was going to have to say about the keys. He'd been tight-lipped all morning, ever since her father had driven him down to look for them on the off chance they might have gotten caught between the rocks. As it turned out, Eve had left them in the ignition, not her pocket. She'd also left the car doors unlocked.

Eve rolled her eyes and turned to her mother in exasperation. "You might as well know the truth. We were having sex on the beach. The tide came in and washed our clothes away. I thought the car keys were in my pocket, so we walked home. I climbed up the trellis and in the bedroom window. You know the rest."

"Fine." Her mother smoothed a hand over the crocheted bedspread. "Don't tell me what you were doing, then. You're an adult. You don't have to explain anything to me."

This was what happened whenever Eve tried to talk to her mother. They ended up angry with each other because her mother didn't want to see the truth, and the truth was, Eve wasn't perfect. Far from it. She did stupid things sometimes. She couldn't be the daughter her mother wanted her to be.

But she would like to end this visit on a different note. Just once it would be nice to part from her mother on good terms. The dolls on the shelves scowled accusingly down at her through their shiny, lifeless eyes. *Say something*, they urged her.

But what?

"Would you mind if I took my dolls home with me?" she asked.

"Do you really want them?" Her mother seemed genuinely pleased. Even after all these years, those dolls still meant something to her. Eve was ashamed she'd only asked for them now because she couldn't think of anything else to say.

"Yes, I really want them." She'd build shelves in the spare room for them. That way, those glassy, lifeless eyes could stare at Matt first thing in the morning. Assuming, of course, Matt still planned on sleeping in the spare room.

Things had gotten very complicated between them. Eve preferred straightforward and simple. She hated this guessing, but she hated having to ask even more.

"I'll get a box for them," her mother said.

Therese hurried out of the room as if afraid Eve might suddenly change her mind, rushing past Matt, who was standing in the hall. The look he gave Eve was warm and approving, and she was suddenly embarrassed to be caught in another sentimental moment.

"Just for that, I'm not going to say anything about the car keys," he told her.

"Thank you."

She wanted to wrap her arms around his big, reassuring body, but was uncertain of her right to do so. They'd agreed on casual. She'd done her part to romance him, just as he'd wanted. She had no idea what their boundaries now were.

They packed the dolls in the box her mother provided,

then Matt carried them to the car.

"I hope you'll be with Eve the next time she comes home," her mother told him as they said their good-byes.

"He might be back in Toronto by then," Eve said to her mother, mainly to see what Matt's reaction would be.

He tucked the box of dolls into the back seat and closed the door. "I'll just have to make sure we visit again before then."

Eve got behind the wheel. Matt seemed preoccupied, and that made her nervous, so she babbled a bit about her work and some of the restoration projects she'd worked on as they drove.

"Historic reconstruction and restoration is a specialty of yours, isn't it?" Matt asked. "I hear there's an art gallery restoration project slated to go ahead for next year. Are you planning to bid on it?"

"I'd like to," Eve said. "But most of that work is done by invitation to tender, and I've never passed their initial screening criteria."

After that, he spoke very little. Instead, he spent most of the drive on his cell phone, talking to Toronto. It was business, and he apologized several times, but consequently, neither one of them was in an especially good mood by the time they reached Halifax that evening.

The city's lights glittered on the black waters of the harbor as they crossed the MacKay Bridge and headed for home. Matt carried their bags and the dolls upstairs, and Eve went outside to drag her compost container to the curb for pickup in the morning.

The neighborhood was quiet.

Then a man stepped into the pale glow from the streetlight at the end of her driveway.

"Hey, Eve," Claude said.

Chapter Thirteen

Matt heard a noise that sounded like a bin overturning and looked out the bedroom window to see what was going on.

Then he heard her shouting his name.

She came from the side of the house, on the driveway, and walked toward the street. Her attention was fastened on a tall man standing under the streetlight on the sidewalk. He wore high-top sneakers, knee-length denim cut-offs, and an orange polo shirt. His hairline started a little farther north of his ears, and the wide smile had been replaced with sulky belligerence, but Matt recognized his face from the newspaper clipping.

Son of a—

He had been entertained when Eve told him how she'd broken her ex-husband's nose and blackened both eyes, but he'd heard about it after the fact, when it was too late to worry and everything had worked out. Now, presented with the very real probability that she'd try it again before he could get there—only this time Claude would be prepared for it—Matt discovered his reaction was different. It bordered on panic. He raced down the stairs and out the front door just in time to see Claude give her a shove.

And Matt saw red.

Yet, as it turned out, she didn't need his protection. In typical Eve style, she didn't waste time on words. She hauled back her arm and swung a punch at her ex-husband, as hard as she could. Claude, however, had indeed been prepared. He turned his head to the side so that the blow glanced off his cheek.

"That was for the phone calls," she was saying, shaking her fingers. "And this," she added, drawing her fist back again, "is for breaking into my house."

There was a fine line between self-defense and assault. Matt caught her around the waist and swung her aside. She kicked out with her feet, trying to free herself, but Matt held on tight.

She stopped struggling. "I'm fine. I'm calm. Really. You can let go of me."

But when Matt did so, she lunged forward. He whipped his arms around her waist again.

"Someone, call the police," Claude was shouting.

Matt didn't understand why the other man wasn't running away. He couldn't hold Eve back much longer. The flashing of red-and-blue lights turning onto the street came almost as a relief. One of the neighbors must have already called in to report a disturbance.

And then, with a sinking sensation in the pit of his stomach, Matt thought he knew what Claude had been trying to accomplish.

"Well, well," said a familiar voice as the officer who had stopped Eve and Matt the night of the fundraiser emerged from the patrol car. He surveyed the scene before him. "You two certainly get around."

· · ·

"Now you know why it's important to keep a record of all the phone calls and the break-ins," Bob said into the silence filling his car.

Did she ever. Eve was still shaking with anger at the injustice of it all. "I can't believe Claude had the nerve to press charges and ask for a peace bond!"

"Don't worry, after a year you can always punch him again. A little jail time won't hurt you," Bob said cheerfully. "And I think you really scared him."

Eve hoped so.

"Thanks for bailing us out," Matt said to his uncle.

"Any time." Bob glanced into his rearview mirror. "You okay back there, Evie?"

"You're enjoying this, aren't you?" she said.

Bob's grin was wide and satisfied. "You bet. More than just a little, too. I'm so proud I might burst into tears. I keep telling you, Evie. You're a bully."

It didn't help any to know she'd proven Bob right. She was, indeed, a bully. If Matt hadn't been having second thoughts about her before, he had to be having them now—even if Claude had deserved another punch in the nose.

Eve slumped back in the cushiony leather seat. But she was feeling just a wee bit frustrated at the reversal of roles. Claude had goaded her into hitting him so he could press charges. Claude had wanted revenge, and she'd let him have it. She hadn't bothered saying that he pushed her first. When Matt tried to clarify that to the police, she'd shut him down.

Now *he* was mad.

"Look on the bright side," Bob added. "Mattie can spend more time on his backlogged business in Toronto. You'll have your house to yourself again. There's the silver lining."

Matt grunted, and Eve contemplated the back of his head. He'd never said a word to her about being backlogged, but what had she thought—that Halifax's pitiful little City Hall was the crowning glory of his illustrious career?

Bob stopped in front of her house.

"By the way, we'll be having an information session at City Hall Wednesday morning. The press will be there." He shot her a thoughtful look over the back of his seat then nudged his nephew. "Seems Evie's friend Marion tipped them off."

"She's not my friend," Eve said. "If you've done something you should be ashamed of, Bob, that's your problem. Not mine. I'm not lying for you."

"Don't worry about it, Eve. You won't have to say a word. Just show up and look beautiful."

Matt dropped his head in his hands. "Don't you know her at all?" Eve heard him mutter to Bob.

Bob sounded surprised. "But she is beautiful."

She was too tired for this. If she had something to say Wednesday morning, she'd say it. There was nothing Bob could do to stop her.

She and Matt walked around to the back of the house and entered through the open deck door. The adrenaline high she'd been on was definitely starting to wear off. She wished he would put his arms around her. She wanted the clock to go back twenty-four hours so they could make love on the beach again. Her heart twisted.

Correction: there had been no talk of love last night, and she wasn't hearing any talk of it now. This was the moment when Matt was supposed to take her in his arms and tell her he wasn't going anywhere, at least not for very long. She counted the ticks of the clock on the wall. *Twenty-seven.* This was awful. She was being needy, and she didn't like the feeling.

Twenty-nine.

"I didn't realize you were falling behind on your work," she said.

"Yes, well." Matt frowned. "That's one of the many things you and I need to talk about."

She had a bad feeling that she wasn't going to like the conversation he had in mind, and decided she didn't want to hear what he had to say. Not yet. Not after tonight.

Not until she'd had more time to prepare herself. She'd been the one to tell him she wanted a casual relationship, and she wasn't going to beg him for more.

"I'm tired," she said. "Can this wait until another time?"

Matt looked like he wanted to argue, then gave in.

"Okay," he said. "But we really need to have a serious talk sometime soon."

Eve needed to have an even more serious talk with herself.

She went to bed, then waited to see where Matt would spend the night. She could hear the low rumble of his voice as he spoke on the phone downstairs. A long while later, he paused for a moment outside her bedroom, then continued down the short hall. His door snicked shut.

Eve rolled over, burying her face in her pillow.

• • •

The next day, Matt was gone before she got home from work. His note said he'd had to make an emergency trip to Toronto, but he'd be back in time for the meeting.

• • •

As she entered City Hall for Bob's meeting on Wednesday morning, he and his uncle were both waiting for her in the main foyer.

It was silly for her heart to pound this way at the sight of him. He'd only been gone two days. Two long, lonely days when she'd buried herself in work, and two longer, lonely nights when she'd stared at her bedroom ceiling, unable to sleep because she was afraid their relationship was over before it had even begun.

Matt, on the other hand, looked like he'd never slept better. It seemed the time they'd been apart hadn't been the agony for him that it had been for her.

"Hey, Eve," he said, kissing her cheek.

She didn't know what to make of that.

"Let's get out of the hallway before the press arrives, shall we?" Bob said to them.

Worn, red carpeting muffled the sounds of their footsteps as Eve hurried to keep up with the longer-legged men. Bob took her elbow and urged her to move faster, but there was already a group of people huddled outside the meeting room.

"Damn." Bob veered down another corridor, dragging Eve with him. "I was hoping to have time to brief you on what to say if you're asked any questions, but I guess I'll just have to trust your judgment."

One of her heels snagged on the carpet and she stumbled.

Matt caught her under the arms from behind. "If you carried her you could make better time," he said to his uncle. "Otherwise, I'd suggest you slow down before she breaks a leg."

"We can do this right here." Bob let go of Eve's arm and she rubbed her elbow, considering all the wonderful ways in which Bob might die. "The Historical Society has raised a—damn," he interrupted himself, swearing again as they all spotted Marion walking toward them. "Marion. How the hell are you this morning?"

If it weren't for Bob's glower, Eve might have thought the two of them were actually glad to see each other.

"Fine, Bob. Just fine." Marion beamed. "The meeting's all

set to begin."

The meeting room was small, filled mostly with a few industry professionals and, of course, the press. Eve recognized some government officials, too.

Marion took a seat beside Bob. "Matt, why don't you start things off with a brief presentation of your design?" she suggested.

Eve was confused. Bob was the mayor. Why was he allowing Marion to take charge of the proceedings?

Matt's presentation was short, to the point, and well-received. Eve still didn't understand what was going on. Anyone could call the city and get this information. What was all the fuss about?

"Is it true that the Historical Society is opposing the destruction of this building?" a reporter asked, his bald head gleaming with sweat.

Bob's response was quick. "Only because the Historical Society hasn't seen the engineer's report condemning this site."

The reporter jotted some notes in his notebook. "Has anyone seen this engineer's report?"

"Of course."

The reporter smiled. "Other than yourself, sir?"

Bob considered the question. "The engineer who wrote it must have seen it," he offered.

There was a ripple of laughter that only served to punctuate the sick feeling Eve now had in the pit of her stomach. She'd seen that report. She might even have mentioned it to Marion, although she couldn't be sure. If she had, it was public information. Marion could have gotten it easily. Eve didn't dare look at Matt. On top of everything else, how would he feel about her if she had somehow done something to ruin his uncle's well-laid plans, even if it hadn't been intentional?

Eve's stomachache worsened.

"There have been reports of expenditures that are grossly over budget," the reporter continued.

Eve leaped to her feet. "I'd like to address that, if I may."

"I'm sorry. You are?" the reporter inquired politely, his pen poised.

"Evangeline Doucette." She spelled her last name. Bob looked like he might be having a stroke. She could see his hands under the table. He was twisting his notes, probably wishing they were her neck. "I'm the project manager. I handle the budget, among other things."

"The budget. Can you explain"—the reporter paused to shuffle through some pages in front of him, then pulled out several photocopied sheets—"an order for twenty custom-made desks at five-thousand dollars apiece, and twenty custom-made chairs, each at a thousand, for the new Council Room, placed before construction has even begun?"

One-hundred-twenty-thousand dollars on furniture.

Eve felt faint. Yes, she could explain it. The high-priced architect shouldn't be left alone with an expense account number and catalogues.

"Custom-made furniture needs to be ordered well in advance," she said. "Those desks and chairs are meant to suit the architectural style of the new building. They are fixtures that will never need to be replaced. As long as the new building stands, any redecorating can be done *around* the furniture and need not *involve* the furniture. Therefore, it will pay for itself in the long run. They'll also make the Council Room an attractive place for tourists to visit. And," she added for good measure, "I'd hardly call them 'grossly over budget.'" She squared her shoulders, aware that Bob and Matt were staring at her in thinly veiled amazement. Well, she wouldn't. She'd call them stupid and frivolous, but she could still see them as assets. She knew her job.

Bob recovered first. "Exactly," he affirmed. "The furniture should be considered permanent fixtures."

"Ms. Doucette." Again, the reporter referred to his notes. Eve was beginning to hate that pile of paper. "Is it true that you are opposed to the demolition of this building?"

Marion was the only person with whom she had discussed the matter, other than Matt and Bob. Whatever happened to professional courtesy?

Or maybe Eve had been too eager to impress her. While she hadn't said anything that wasn't public information, it still made her feel like she'd done something underhanded.

"I work for the contractor on the new construction," she explained. She fought an urge to wipe her damp hands on something, like maybe Bob for dragging her into this mess. "The demolition of the current Hall has nothing to do with my position as project manager for the new structure."

"Do you specialize in historical restorations?"

This reporter had certainly come prepared. She suspected that his hesitancy over her name had only been for effect. What had Marion told him?

"I have worked on restoration projects, yes." She now had a good idea where this conversation was going, and since the reporter knew exactly who she was, telling lies could only harm her professional integrity. Telling the truth, however, might possibly harm Bob, and through him, Matt. "But that's not what I was hired for on this project."

"Have you seen the engineer's report Mayor Anderson referred to?"

Everyone in the room waited for her answer. "Yes, I have."

"What's your professional opinion on it?"

"I have no professional opinion. I haven't enough

information to give one."

"Then what about a personal opinion?"

Bob sprang to his feet. "I think Ms. Doucette has already told you that she hasn't formed an opinion. She's not an engineer or an architect. I can't imagine how her opinion would be of value."

Couldn't imagine how her opinion would be of value? If Eve were to kill him, she had a room full of witnesses who could swear she'd been driven to it.

"Sir," the reporter replied politely, "it's my understanding that she has, indeed, formed an opinion. Furthermore, it is also my understanding that she is fully qualified to state that opinion." He proceeded to list Eve's qualifications, and Eve had to admit, she did sound impressive. "Now, Ms. Doucette. Can this building be saved? And if so, would saving it be economically feasible?"

"I don't think it's fair to put Ms. Doucette on the spot like this," Bob continued to protest. "We're here to talk about the new construction, not the old building."

The reporter scented blood in the water. "Are you saying that Ms. Doucette is not allowed to answer my question?"

Bob straightened his shoulders and looked at Eve. "I'm advising against it."

Eve now had to make a choice. Everyone in the room knew that Bob Anderson was trying to pull something. Did she let him get away with it, or did she give her honest opinion? Eve asked herself what her response would be if it weren't for Matt.

But Matt had never given her any reason to think she couldn't be honest. She wouldn't want him this much if he had.

"Yes," she answered slowly. "I think it would be possible to save this building. But without doing cost estimates, I have no idea whether or not it would be feasible for the city to do so."

The reporter grunted, then moved on to other victims, for which Eve was thankful.

Bob seemed displeased, but she didn't especially care since she wasn't pleased with him, either. She did, however, care about Matt. His expression was unreadable, his whole attention seemingly now focused on the next speaker, and she tried not to feel hurt.

She'd been asked for her professional opinion, and she'd given it. She couldn't have done anything else, not even for Matt. Because regardless of what others thought, it was more important to her that she approve of herself.

That was the mistake she'd made in marrying Claude. She'd thought he was more important than she was, simply because they'd both been impressed by his doctorate degree.

When the meeting was over she gathered her things and rushed from the room, ignoring the reporters who called out for her to wait.

• • •

Eve took off so fast, Matt couldn't stop her.

He wanted to go after her, but his issues with his uncle weren't going to wait. He'd catch up with Eve as soon as he could because they had things to discuss, too, but he was tired of people messing with her. That included his uncle. She was so easily manipulated, and never seemed to see it coming.

Claude had manipulated her, too. Eve hadn't gone to the police before, and he'd known she wouldn't this time. He'd anticipated that she'd try and hit him again, and he'd done his best to provoke her. That was why he'd turned his head away. He'd planned all along to press charges against her.

Because Eve was far more predictable than she realized.

Matt leaned closer so only Uncle Bob could hear. "I want to see you in your office."

His uncle froze for a millisecond, then continued to toss notes back into his briefcase. "Not now, Mattie. I have damage control to attend to."

"If you don't find the time right this minute, you're going to have a lot more damage than this to control."

Uncle Bob spoke up, addressing a few of the reporters who were hovering near the door. "I can't talk right now," he said. "A family emergency has just come up."

Matt followed close behind him. They strode down the hall and up the wide staircase, then turned right into a suite of offices. Packing crates littered the floors.

Uncle Bob waved to his secretary. "Hold my calls."

He closed the heavy, colonial door leading to his private office before facing Matt. "Can we make this fast? I really do have things I need to take care of. That meeting was a total disaster."

For a man who thought the meeting was such a *disaster*, Uncle Bob wasn't looking all that upset. In fact, he was looking downright happy.

"I hope you aren't planning to blame this on Eve," Matt said quietly.

"Not at all. If there's one thing that can be counted on in this world, it's that Evie will do exactly what she thinks is right." His uncle rubbed his hands together. "People expect me to try and pull something over on them, and she just proved them correct. Always give people what they expect, Mattie. Remember that. Keeps them on their toes. Thanks to her, between the money we've already raised and the money the province will now have to kick in to protect a heritage site, we can build one helluva Matt Brison original."

"You used Eve to get what you want," Matt said. Eve might be wrong about his uncle being a moron, but Uncle Bob was something, all right. "Plus, you insulted her professionalism. Do you even care how you made her feel today?"

"I'll make it up to her."

Matt wondered what world his uncle lived in. "If I were you, I wouldn't send her flowers. Perhaps you haven't noticed, but she doesn't like them very much."

"No, I won't send her flowers. But I have arranged for her ex-husband to be sent on a special long-term research project in the Arctic Ocean," Bob said. "Good thing Evie got in that punch when she did. Seems the federal government needs a shellfish expert, and the University's president highly recommended him for the position." Uncle Bob, whistling merrily, sank an imaginary putt. "You should take up golf, Mattie. You get to be friends with a lot of influential people."

From the South Pacific to hunting shellfish in the Arctic... ouch. That would have to hurt almost as much as Claude's broken nose. Uncle Bob was a man who really knew how to throw a punch.

In that instant, Matt forgave him. "Thank you," he said. He'd been grateful before for the things his uncle had done for him over the years, but this trumped them all. "I don't know how to repay you."

"A private donation would be nice. Eve's been making noise about wanting me to buy curtains for a youth Internet café project she's been volunteering on." Bob looked at him thoughtfully for a long moment. "I keep trying to tell you that she's too good for you."

"She is, but I'm going to marry her, anyway." All he had to do was figure out some way to get her to say yes. Deep down, tough little Eve was scared to death of commitment.

Uncle Bob shifted some papers on his desk, a small,

satisfied smile lurking on his lips. "Finally. I was starting to worry you'd never figure out that smart men marry up."

Matt knew he'd been played. He supposed he'd known all along. "What makes you think she'll marry down?"

"I told you already. If there's one thing you can count on, it's that Eve will do what she thinks is right." Uncle Bob's smile widened. "And what she thinks is right is usually the opposite of whatever I say."

Chapter Fourteen

Marion pushed open the front door of City Hall and stepped out into blazing sunlight behind Eve. "Bob's not above the law," she said. "He can't just go around imploding heritage sites because it suits his purposes."

Eve tried to calm herself. "I don't want to be a part of your strategy for putting Bob in his place." Not if it meant hurting Matt.

"Yet, you came off looking great," Marion said. "You'll get your name—and your credentials—in the press. That'll be a big help to you when the Province buys the old Hall from the Municipality. We're going to restore it." Eve could hear the satisfaction in the other woman's voice. "You'll be invited to submit a tender—I'll see that you are. And Bob's still going to get his new Hall. It just won't be on the site he wants. What's not to like?"

Eve went hot, then cold. This explained Matt's silence in the car on their way home from her parents' place. Somehow he had known about this, even though she hadn't, which meant he'd heard it from Bob. Not only had he gotten dragged to the police station over what they'd classified as a domestic dispute because of her, but Matt probably thought she was a liar now, too. And there was no guarantee she'd even be given the work.

"You might as well get used to this." Marion's tone was kind, although her words were heartless. "This is business, and Bob took his chances. Besides, I wouldn't be too sure this isn't exactly what he wanted."

Marion was undoubtedly right. It wouldn't surprise Eve at all if Bob had planned things this way. His underhandedness knew no bounds.

Marion got into a waiting taxi, giving Eve a friendly wave as she rode off.

Eve had no idea what to do next, only that she wasn't yet ready to face Matt. Suddenly, he was there, anyway, behind her on the steps, his expression intent. Determined.

And focused on her.

She knew that look all too well. Right away, it put her on the defensive.

"I had to tell the truth in there," she said, cutting him off before he could get a word in. "I'm sorry if I made things more difficult for your uncle, but Bob doesn't seem to know the difference between right and wrong."

"I don't think you need to feel too sorry for Uncle Bob," Matt said, although his expression never altered. He looked around at the busy street. "But there's something I need to talk to you about, and this isn't exactly private."

If he planned to lecture her, she wasn't ready to hear it. "I've got to go. I have to get to a job site."

"Eve, wait. I—"

She scurried down the stairs but didn't get farther than the gated street entry to the front courtyard before a shrill whistle rent the air.

"Hey, baby! Bring some of that over here!"

Eve froze.

Matt?

There were a few reporters milling around on the front steps of the Hall, as well as a camera crew and several tourists, not to mention the people out on the street. Yet that had come from Matt?

"Never mind. I'll come and get it myself," he said, jogging past the press and down the steps toward her. The next thing she knew he'd hoisted her over his shoulder, planting his hand on her backside to keep her short skirt in place. Her briefcase went flying.

"Put me down," she hissed, all the blood rushing to her head in her upside-down position. She tried to brush her hair out of her eyes.

Matt stooped and grabbed her briefcase. "This is the only thing you seem to understand," he said. "But I've got to say, I thought you were better than this." He steadily ignored the laughter as he carried her back up the steps. "I never realized you were such a coward that you'd spend the rest of your life afraid to try again."

"I have no idea what you're talking about," she said. She must look really stupid hanging over Matt's shoulder with his hand patting her—

"I think you do." Someone opened the door for him and he thanked him or her politely, as if it were natural to be hauling a woman around like a sack of cement. He climbed the stairs to the second floor and searched for an empty room. When he found one, he shut the door behind them and lowered her to her feet. He set her briefcase on a desk.

"I know you aren't crazy about the idea of a long-term commitment, but I think there's something you should know. Sooner or later, I'm going to marry you. I'll give you plenty of time to get used to the idea, but once you do, I want you to understand that this marriage is going to last a whole lot longer than two weeks. So don't even think about sending the gifts back."

He was serious.

"I drive you crazy," she said, refusing to believe it. He couldn't have thought this through. "I'm always going to say or do exactly what I think. I'll never make you happy."

"I don't want to be happy. I want you." He was grinning like a nut. "I never got to finish the list of things I like about you. Where was I? Oh, yeah. Professional. I like your honesty. I like the way you always do what you believe is right, even if it turns out you're wrong. And personal. I love you. All of you, even the irritating bits, and not just those skimpy little panties you leave hanging all over the place. I want to marry you, Eve. I want to have babies with you."

He'd said he loved her.

Her heartstrings were now strung so tight there was a real possibility she might be having a heart attack. Then, the rest of what he'd said registered.

Babies. Matt definitely hadn't thought this through.

"It's hard enough to get out of a mistake when there are just two people involved," she pointed out. "It would be impossible if there were children. We'd be stuck with each other forever."

"'Stuck' isn't the word I'd use, but I'm willing to take that chance. I know the whole idea of marriage scares you, but I'll be right there with you, helping you out."

"What if we change?" she asked, wanting to make sure he knew what he was getting himself into, afraid to let herself hope too much. "What if in five years' time we aren't the same people anymore?"

"Of course we won't be the same people," he said. "People grow and change. But we'll be growing and changing together."

She thought about what marriage to Matt would mean. It meant children—which she thought she'd enjoy—although now that he'd met her family and seen the gene pool, he couldn't possibly want more than one or two. It meant starting her career over and moving to Toronto, because she couldn't see the practical sense in having him be the one to try and move a whole business to Nova Scotia.

It meant loving him as much as he loved her. Or, possibly, even a little bit more, because Eve suddenly realized something. If Matt had been the one to ask her to move to a small island in the South Pacific, she'd have followed him gladly. She'd follow him anywhere. Yet here she was, pushing him away when what she should be doing was hanging on as tight as she possibly could.

She could do commitment. She'd simply needed to find the right person to trust with her heart.

"Are you going to make me live in a house made of glass and steel?" she asked.

"I don't think putting you in a glass house is such a good idea," he replied, a slow smile easing his intensity. "I was picturing something like an old farmhouse we could renovate together. Something with lots of room for a homegrown soccer team."

Okay, so maybe he would want more than one or two children—and it didn't make sense to waste all that space he was talking about, did it?

Eve buried herself in his arms.

"In that case," she said, "I'm all yours. I love you, too, Matt."

"If you love me, you're going to have to stop referring to marriage as a mistake," he said, seconds before his lips closed over hers. "Because personally, I've never made a mistake that feels this right."

And Eve, safely cocooned as she was in the warmth and love of his embrace, found herself inclined to agree.

Acknowledgments

The team at Entangled Publishing is fabulous. Thanks to all of them, especially Danielle Poiesz for her editing skills.

I'd also like to thank Andrea Fox, who's the construction project manager in the family, and Stella MacLean, Anne MacFarlane, and Victoria LeBlanc for being first readers. I have the best family and friends.

About the Author

Paula Altenburg grew up in rural Nova Scotia knowing that at some point in her life she was likely to be a fiction writer. Swapping Louis L'Amour and Zane Grey books with her father guaranteed she wasn't going to be the next Jane Austen, much to the dismay of her English teacher mother.

A degree in Social Anthropology from the University of King's College and Dalhousie University in Halifax, Nova Scotia, again meant writing was the logical (meaning only) career path for her, although it did confirm her belief that learning is a life-long experience. She's taken business courses, writing courses, and physiology of aquatic animals courses, all at the university level and all for fun.

She has worked in the Aerospace industry, which surprises everyone who knows her, although now makes writing her fulltime career. Happily married, with two terrific sons, she continues to live in rural Nova Scotia but makes a point of traveling as much as she can.

She reads in all genres, which isn't surprising considering her life is all over the board, but fantasy and paranormal romance are her writing loves.

Paula also co-authors paranormal romance under the pseudonym Taylor Keating.

Visit her at www.paulaaltenburg.com.

Find your Bliss with these new releases...

***Kissing the Maid of Honor* by Robin Bielman**
Sela Sullivan is resolved to be the best maid of honor ever, even if it means tolerating the best man. Arrogant Luke Watters is not only the guy who humiliated her at a kissing booth in high school, but he also happens to be her best friend's older brother. Luke can't deny Sela inspires a passion he's never known, but can he prove to the maid of honor he's become a man of honor?

***Tempting Cameron* by Karen Erickson**
For Cameron McKenzie, resident good girl Chloe Dawson has always just been his younger sister Jane's best friend. It isn't until Jane's wedding that Chloe reappears in his life—and the beautiful woman now tempts him beyond reason. Chloe's always dreamed of a future with the dark, brooding Cam, so she makes him an offer: one sweet summer romance with no strings attached. This good girl's ready for an adventure—one that just might last a lifetime.

***Real Men Don't Quit* by Coleen Kwan**
When famous author Luke Maguire decides to write his next novel in the small town of Burronga, Australia, he's sure he can ignore Tyler, the fiery redhead next door. Only Tyler and Luke can't stay away from each other. So they set rules. No staying overnight, no future plans, no sappy good-byes when Luke inevitably quits town. But the chemistry between them is too strong to contain in a rulebook. Are Luke and Tyler ready to risk their lives of independence for something more?

***Construction Beauty Queen* by Sara Daniel**
Chicago socialite Veronica Jamison heads to her grandfather's small town of Kortville, ready to roll up her sleeves and work for the family construction business. Matt Shaw just wants to run his business, not manage a spoiled-rotten princess he knows he'll never be good enough for. With the quirky townspeople rallying against Veronica inheriting her grandfather's business, it's up to Matt to try to drive her out of town. But how can he, when instead she's driving her way into his heart?

Made in the USA
Charleston, SC
17 November 2013